We stood in the darkness a
before I rang the bell again. Sudd
flooded the porch, and the door flew open. We to͟s͟e͟
flour and bolted down the steps. I remember seeing a startled man with flour on his legs and shoes. I heard him yell,
and a woman saying, "I'll get 'em!:

As I ran, I glanced back and saw her chasing us. We
were far ahead and would have made it safely out of the
yard if I hadn't gone and tripped. I went sprawling, and a
sharp pain shot into my knee.

Susan stopped beside me. I sat up and grabbed at
my knee, fighting back tears.

"Whadya guys think you're doing!" yelled the
woman, who had caught up with us. She yanked at my
arm.

I struggled to my feet, and as I did, my hat fell off.
She let go of my arm.

"Why," she said, "you're a girl!"

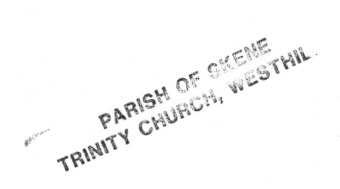

Be sure to read all of the
books in the Chronicles
of Courage series:

A Better Tomorrow?

Operation Morningstar

Gold in the Garden

Gold in
the Garden

Gold in the Garden

Dorothy Lilja Harrison

Chariot VICTOR
PUBLISHING
A DIVISION OF COOK COMMUNICATIONS

Chariot Books
is an imprint of ChariotVictor Publishing, a division of Cook
Communications, Colorado Springs, Colorado 80918
Cook Communications, Paris, Ontario
Kingsway Communications, Eastbourne, England

GOLD IN THE GARDEN
© 1997 by Dorothy Lilja Harrison

Cover design by Rick A. Mills
Cover illustration by Ron Mazellan

First printing, 1997
Printed in the United States of America
01 00 99 98 97   5 4 3 2 1

To my husband, the Rev. Dr. Clifford Harrison,
whose gentle faith continually inspires me,
and whose keen insights as a hospice chaplain
were invaluable to me as I created this book.

Table of Contents

Acknowledgments

I am deeply grateful to Dr. Lauro Halstead of the National Rehabilitation Hospital, Washington, D.C., for his kindness in answering my questions regarding the incubation period, onset, and symptoms of poliomyelitis as I wrote the story and the section concerning polio epidemics. A reknowned authority on this devastating disease, he gave wise counsel and valuable corrections, which ensured that the information I have presented is scientifically accurate.

I am also indebted to the Office of Communications, National Institute of Allergy and Infectious Diseases (one of the National Institutes of Health in Bethesda, Md.) for supplying supplementary material on the history of polio in the United States.

And I gained much in my conversations with my friend, Dottie Harper, who survived polio as an infant and whose courageous struggle now with post-polio syndrome is an inspiration to all whose lives she touches.

Chapter 1

1952

Death was something I'd never thought about very much. No one I knew had ever died—at least, not in the four years since we'd moved to Maryland. I had passed the Curtis Funeral Home almost every day since then, but this was the first time I'd ever actually gone there.

The parking lot was filling up fast, but luckily my dad found a space under a tree so the car wouldn't heat up as much while we were inside. All four of us were sweating, and it was only 10:30 in the morning.

"Leave the windows open a crack," said Daddy, pulling on the emergency brake.

Jeremy looked over at me. "Lets the air circulate," he said, as if I didn't know it. He's two years older than I am, and he thinks I don't know anything.

My mother was the first one out of the car. She leaned into the open window on my side and gave me the same look that she does when I've been home sick and she's not sure I'm ready to go back to school. "Are you *sure* you want to go through this, Kathy?"

I glared at her as I cranked up the window. "Susan's my best friend, Mother."

"I know, but you didn't go to the viewing, and . . ."

"You wouldn't *let* me," I snapped, pushing the door open. She hadn't wanted me to go to the funeral, either. Probably afraid I'd make a scene or something.

Daddy spoke to Mother over his shoulder. "Leave her alone, Marge," he said quietly.

We crossed the blistering parking lot, Daddy and Jeremy first, with Mother and me following after. Mother tried to reach for my hand, but I pulled away. I was thinking about Susan and how she had told me that someone had fried an egg on the sidewalk down the street from us. "We could open a restaurant right here," she'd giggled.

"Yeah," I had said, "the Valley Green Sidewalk Cafe. Eggs cooked to order while the '52 heat wave lasts!"

That was two weeks ago. Just two weeks . . .

We reached the green canopied walkway that led up the marble steps to a pillared front porch. A solemn-faced man dressed in a dark suit stood next to the broad front entrance. He shook hands with my father and stepped aside to let us enter.

My stomach knotted up a little when the door opened, so I let the others go first. To my surprise, though, the room inside didn't look much different than a living room. A lady in a gray lace dress sat at a bare desk fanning herself. She smiled faintly as Mother approached.

"We're here for the Marshall service," said Mother.

"That's in the Parlor of Peace," answered the lady, in a soft voice. "Down the hall—first door to the left."

As it turned out, she didn't have to tell us. The carpeted hallway was crowded with people I knew—a lot of them were kids from my seventh-grade class. Some of my teachers were there, too. I'd never seen them outside of school before, and certainly never on a Saturday in August.

The whole thing seemed unreal. I kept wishing I could wake up and find it was just a dream.

In the next room, a pearl-white coffin stood along a back wall. The hinged lid, propped open like the cover of a jewelry box, was lined with white satin. I was glad I couldn't see the inside from where I stood. Baskets of flowers—pink and white and yellow—were stacked up like a soft wall on both sides. As much as I love flowers, the sickening sweet smell of so many piled together made my stomach turn, even though a room air conditioner purred somewhere behind me.

Mother nodded toward the coffin, but I shook my head, so the three of them got in line without me. I found a place to stand near the back, in the shadow of a potted palm, and I waited, weak-kneed and hoping I wouldn't throw up. One by one, my classmates inched past the casket. Some of the girls were crying.

Mr. and Mrs. Marshall stood quietly nearby shaking hands with people. I had hardly ever seen them when they weren't smiling or laughing, so they didn't seem real either. And for the first time I had no idea what to say to them. They had always been like second parents to me. I called them "Ma and Pa Marshall" for fun, and they called me their "other child." How could I ever talk to them again? What would I say?

Rows of folding chairs took up the rest of the room. I saved four seats and was grateful when my family settled down around me. Having them nearby helped.

I don't remember much of what our minister said during the service, but I remember he stopped once and wiped his eyes. I know he read the Twenty-third Psalm, though, because that's when everything got blurry and Jeremy offered me his handkerchief. Susan and I had memorized that psalm last year in Sunday school.

When the service was over, everyone stood up to leave. I looked up at Mother. "When do they close it?" I asked softly.

"The coffin?"

"Yes."

"Very soon." She looked at me closely. "Do you want to go up now?"

I thought for a moment, and then I nodded. This would be my last chance to see her. I slid past Mother and Daddy and managed to make it up there by keeping my head down.

When I reached the coffin, I looked up—and there was Susan. Only it wasn't her. She looked like a dummy from a wax museum or something. Her hair was the same, but they had put powder on her face, and lipstick. Lipstick! I bit my lip and felt my eyes fill up. Susan would never just lie there all made up and not peek at me—and maybe wink. This person was as quiet as a stone and just as cold, probably.

Someone had put a white rose into her still, folded hands. I leaned closer so I could see it better. The flower was real. The only real thing in that box. The rest of it was just pretend. *Oh, please, God, make it pretend! And don't let anyone know that it was me, Kathy Jordan—her best friend—that made her die.*

Chapter 2

1952

I had met Susan Marshall almost four years earlier at Valley Green, the elementary school most of the kids in our housing development attended. That was in September of 1948, and we had just moved into our new house in the Valley Green subdivision. I was dreading the first day of school, thinking I might be the only new kid in fourth grade.

My mother knew better. "You won't be the only one," she said at breakfast, watching me sulk over my cereal. "You just watch. There'll be other new children."

It turned out there were five new kids in my class alone, and one of them was Susan. The first time I talked to her was that morning at recess. I was sitting on the monkey bars, wishing someone would ask me to play dodge ball, like some of the kids were doing.

"Where are you from?" Susan asked, climbing up next to me.

I looked over at her. "New Jersey," I said. "How about you?"

Susan let go and hung by her knees. "We just moved here from New London."

"Where's that?" I said. New London sounded like it

might be across the ocean or something.

She swung back up, looking surprised. "Connecticut, of course." Then she smiled. "My father was in the Navy."

"Oh," I said, swinging down like Susan had just done. "Mine was in the Air Force." My skirt fell over my eyes, so I swung back up as fast as I could.

"You like our teacher?" she asked.

"She's okay. But Miss Robbins—my second-grade teacher—she was the best!" I didn't say how I'd cried when we had to move halfway through that year. We had moved so often, I was used to it, but I still hated it. I was always saying good-bye to my friends.

Susan, of course, had spent her life near military bases too. "Now that we're in Valley Green, though," she told me, "my mother doesn't ever want to move again." She tossed her dark ponytail. "And neither do I!"

I smiled. "Me neither," I said. "My mother and I are sick of moving, and my father said buying our house was something he thought about all the time he was in the war."

The bell rang, so we jumped down from the monkey bars and filed back into the building together. We sat next to each other at lunch, and after school we walked home together.

"Can you come over and play later?" asked Susan, when we got to her house. "I've got a new jigsaw puzzle."

I shook my head. "Not today. My mother wants me and Jeremy to finish unpacking our rooms."

"That your brother?" asked Susan.

I rolled my eyes. "Yeah."

"Lucky you," she said. "I don't have any brothers or sisters."

"You can have Jeremy anytime you want him," I laughed. "Big brothers are a pain." Then I said, "Want me to stop by for you tomorrow morning?"

"Sure!"

"Okay! See you at about 8:15," I called over my shoulder, and then I skipped the remaining two blocks down to my house. This is going to be a fun place to live, I thought. At last I can have a real best friend!

I made other friends in the weeks that followed, of course, but Susan was the one I liked best. Our families had even joined the same church—Madison Memorial Methodist, just down the street from where we lived. Susan and I were in the same Sunday School class, which met in a trailer on the church parking lot. Across from the small building near the little white framed church, was a huge, deep hole. "Someday that will be the basement of the new building," Daddy had told me. "Then you'll have a real Sunday School classroom." Towers of cinder blocks and bricks stood near the hole, ready to be put into place.

"Madison Memorial Church is growing by leaps and bounds," my mother said at breakfast one Sunday morning.

"Yep," said my dad, stirring his coffee. "The farmers who started it would be amazed to see it now." Our little white frame church building was almost a hundred years old. We had to have three services every Sunday morning, with so many members. Even so, folding chairs usually crowded the aisles.

"We're so lucky to have Phil Thomas for our preacher," said my mother, clearing the table. "I hope he stays here a long time—at least until our new church building is finished."

My dad wasn't so sure it was Mr. Thomas' preaching that brought in the crowds. He said it was mostly because of all the new families moving in. "Phil was just in the right place at the right time," he said. And that's how I felt about myself, having found Susan for a friend. I knew I had been "in the right place at the right time."

In October Susan told me she was going to join the junior choir. She had sung in one when she lived up in New London. "It was lots of fun," she said. "You want to be in it, too? We're going to practice on Wednesdays after school."

I loved to sing, but I shook my head. "I can't read music," I said.

"That's okay," she said. "You won't have to."

I went with Susan to the first choir practice. We got there early, so we stood around outside with some other kids from our class until Mrs. Fritz, the choir director, arrived. Before she did, though, two older girls came up to us. "What do you sing?" one of them asked me.

I looked up at her. "Oh, just about anything," I said innocently.

She glanced at the other girl, and they both snickered. "I mean," she said, "what part?"

I shrugged, not knowing what a "part" was. I could feel my cheeks burning.

The other girl rolled her eyes and turned her back to me.

Susan slipped her arm around my waist and tossed her head. "Kathy's a soprano," she said, "just like me!" I knew then that she was my best friend ever.

Later, Mrs. Fritz took down our names and phone numbers, and she asked each of us what part we sang. When it was my turn, Susan winked at me as I spoke right up. "I'm a soprano!" I said. And that's how I got to sit in the front row with Susan.

Mrs. Fritz had orange hair and tiny glasses, which were perched on the end of her nose. When she stood up in front of the room and peered at us over the glasses, all of our chattering stopped. Even the boys were quiet.

"All right now, children," she said, with a merry twinkle in her eyes, "let's warm up!" I quickly learned that "warm up" meant getting our voices ready to sing. First she had us sing a scale, each note higher than the last: "Do, re, mi, fa, sol, la, ti, do." She raised her hands with each note until they were high above her head. Then they slowly lowered as we sang back down the scale: "Do, ti, la, sol, fa, mi, re, do!"

"Excellent!" she said, pushing her glasses back into place. "Now do it again, but this time, on each note, sing 'Nee, nay, new, no, nah!'" And so we did, all the way up the scale and back down again. Some of us started to giggle as we sang, but Mrs. Fritz said, "Wonderful! You sound almost like the adult choir!"

I loved being a real choir member and singing in church, and I loved Mrs. Fritz, too. Everybody did.

Each week at practice I listened hard to the sopranos around me, and pretty soon I knew all the songs they did. But I also listened to the kids in the row behind us. They sang some of the songs on lower notes than we did. Mrs. Fritz called them "altos" and said they were singing the "harmony." We sopranos, she had told us, were singing the "melody." I secretly wished I could sing the harmony, too, even if I had to sit with the altos.

A few days later Susan and I were singing together at her house while we were cutting out paper dolls. Suddenly she stopped singing right in the middle of "Blue Skies," a song we had heard a lot on the radio. "Why don't you sing the high notes?" she said.

I grinned. "I can't sing that high."

"Maybe you should be an alto."

"I wish I could, but they have to read music," I said.

"Then I'll teach you!"

And she did. She started that very day. She flipped through the hymn book on the piano and opened it to "Away in a Manger."

I giggled. "That's a Christmas carol," I said.

"So what? It's easier to follow the notes if you know the tune." Susan was right. By studying the songs I already knew, reading the notes was easy.

Mrs. Marshall came through the living room while we were at the piano. She had dark hair like Susan's and the same eyes. I thought when I saw her that Susan would probably look just like her mother when she was grown up. "If you'd like, Kathy," said Mrs. Marshall, "you're welcome to take the hymnbook home with you for a few days."

"Wow, that would be great!" I said, cradling the book. "We don't have one of these at our house." And in a few days, by practicing at home, I learned some brand new hymns.

The next time I was at Susan's, her mother played some of the hymns on the piano for us. "You girls sing well together," she said. "Want to try some harmonizing?"

Susan and I looked at each other. "Sure!" we said. So while Mrs. Marshall played "Away in a Manger," the two of us sang along, with me reading the alto. We harmonized all the way to the end of the carol. And not long after that Mrs. Fritz let me sing alto in the choir!

Another time when Susan and I were singing with her mother, Mrs. Marshall said, "Let's try 'Depth of Mercy.' That's one of my favorites."

As soon as she started playing the hymn, I remembered hearing it in church. "I like the melody," I said, "but not some of the words." I wrinkled my nose.

"Yeah," said Susan, "the line that says 'Me, the chief

of sinners . . .' Who wrote that, anyway?"

Susan's mother smiled. "Someone in the Bible said it first, but you can always find the name of a hymn writer printed next to the hymn." She pointed. "See, this one was written by Charles Wesley."

"Oh," I said, "we learned about Wesley in Sunday School. He started the Methodist Church!"

"No," she said, "that was his brother, John."

I frowned. "Was Charles a bad guy?"

Mrs. Marshall smiled again. "Maybe he was once, but later, after he was forgiven, he wrote over a thousand hymns!"

They let me borrow the hymn book again, and that night I practiced "Depth of Mercy" after supper. I liked the third verse better than the first, especially at the end, where it said, "Jesus weeps and loves me still." How could a guy who was "the chief of sinners" say that? I wondered. Little did I know that someday I'd feel that way, too.

Chapter 3

1952

The following fall, when Susan and I were in the fifth grade, we decided to start a girls' club. "We're going to meet every Monday after school," I told Jeremy and my mother one morning at breakfast.

"Where?" asked mother, pushing bread slices down into the toaster.

I set down my juice glass. "I thought maybe we could meet at our house—now that Daddy's finished the rec room."

Mother turned and faced me. "How many kids?"

I shrugged. "Depends. It's just for certain people."

Jeremy sat pouring catsup on his fried egg. "Yeah," he said, "you have to be ugly to join."

I stuck out my tongue at him, and then I continued, "It's just for girls whose fathers were in the war."

Mother smiled. "That might well be half of the school."

"They have to be in fifth grade," I said. "No one else is allowed!"

Seven kids from my class showed up for the first meeting: Jeannie Grayson; Sheila Wilkins; Phyllis Webster;

Beverly Baker; the Moberg twins, Mollie and Millie; and, of course, Susan. My mother had refreshments ready for us on the kitchen table when we got to my house.

"Oh, boy!" said Mollie. "Cupcakes!"

"And green Kool-Aid!" said her sister.

Mother smiled. "In honor of the charter members," she said.

"Who's that?" asked Beverly.

"All of you," she said, placing some paper napkins next to the stack of plates. "The first members of any club are called the 'charter members.'"

"Wow," said Susan. "That sounds important!" And we all agreed as we helped ourselves.

After we finished our cupcakes and all the Kool-Aid was gone, we went downstairs to our rec room to hold the meeting. The first thing we did was to think up a name for our club.

"It should say who can be members," said Phyllis.

"Yeah," said Sheila. "Something like the Veterans' Kids."

I shook my head. "That sounds like boys can join, too."

Everyone groaned at that, so we changed it to the Veterans' Girls. But that sounded like we were their girl-friends.

Susan said, "How about Daughters of the Veterans?" and that sounded fine to everyone.

Next came the election of officers. "I'd like to nominate Kathy for president," said Phyllis.

I grinned and crossed my fingers. I really wanted to be president.

"I second the motion!" said Millie.

There was silence for a few moments. Finally, I nominated Jeannie, just to be polite and not because I wanted anyone else to win but me. When Jeannie shot me a look that said "thanks," though, I felt guilty.

"How are we going to vote?" asked Susan.

"How else? By raising our hands, of course," said Beverly.

Susan shook her head. "I think it should be by secret ballot."

"What's that?" said Millie, raising her eyebrows.

Susan grinned. "Everyone writes who they want on a slip of paper."

"Yeah," said Sheila. "Then you fold up your paper so no one can see who you voted for."

We all agreed that that was the way to do it. And it sounded especially good to me, because then I could vote for myself. *After all,* I thought, *if I want to be president, why vote for anyone else? Besides,* I told myself, *I was the one who had started the club, so I deserve it.*

I ran and got some pencils from around the house, and Mother gave me some paper to tear into smaller pieces. They were just large enough for us to write down the name of our candidate.

Susan wanted to count the ballots, since it had been her idea. Soberly, we each dropped them into a bowl my mother gave us. Then Susan took them into the laundry room to count them. When she returned, she smiled, cleared her throat loudly, and said, "The winner is Kathy Jordan!"

Everybody applauded except for Jeannie, and I grinned shyly, hoping I didn't look as happy as I felt. In a few minutes, though, even Jeannie was calling me "Madam President." I loved every minute of it. *And after all,* I told myself, *I was the one whose mother had baked the cupcakes.*

Susan was the last to leave that afternoon because

she stayed to help me tidy up. Before she left, she remembered to go back into the laundry room to get the ballots. When she came back, though, she was empty-handed.

"Where are the ballots?" I asked.

"In the wastebasket next to the washer," she said, and I nodded.

When we were finished, I walked her halfway home, like we always did when we played at each other's houses. As we parted, Susan said, "Well, 'bye Prexy."

"Prexy?"

"Nickname for president. My dad told me."

I grinned.

"You really wanted that job, didn't you?" said Susan.

"What do you mean?"

"Oh, nothing," she said, walking off.

As soon as I got back home, I ran downstairs and pulled the ballots out of the wastebasket, tucking them into my pocket. Then, safely up in my room, I spread all eight slips out on my bed. I recognized Susan's handwriting, of course, and a couple of the others. All eight said the same thing: "Kathy."

I bit my lip. So Susan knew I had voted for myself, even though I had nominated Jeannie. Deep down inside, though, I was still glad I had won, no matter what. And Susan never let on that she knew. That's the kind of friend she was.

When the Daughters of the Veterans met the following week, we started off by singing some service songs, like "Anchors Aweigh" and "The Caissons Go Rolling Along."

When we finished, I said quickly, "How about the Air Force song—for my father?" So we sang that, too, and later "The Marine's Hymn" for someone else. We had learned the words to most of the songs in school, but we also heard them played on the radio all the time.

When we got tired of singing, we each bragged about where our fathers had served, even if we didn't know much about it.

"Was your father a pilot?" Beverly asked me.

"Uh-uh," I said. "A bombardier."

"Where did he drop bombs?"

"German cities, mostly, but he never talks about it." *Except in his sleep,* I thought. I still heard him yell sometimes in the middle of the night.

Beverly nodded soberly. "I know what you mean. My uncle used to wear his combat boots all the time—even to bed!"

Sheila joined in. "My father couldn't even sleep in a bed—or any place soft like that." She told us how he slept on the floor for weeks because he had gotten so used to sleeping on the hard ground in a foxhole.

By the third meeting, we were running out of things to say about being daughters of veterans. By the fourth meeting, only three kids showed up besides me: Susan, Phyllis, and Sheila.

"I know two other kids who want to join," said Phyllis, "Donna Graham and Nancy Callahan."

"They can't," said Sheila. "I don't think their fathers are veterans."

"Yeah, but they're so much fun!"

There was silence for a few moments. Then I leaned back and said, "We could change our name."

"What?" said everyone.

"You know, stand for something different," I said.

"Like what?" they wanted to know.

I shrugged and it was quiet again, and then someone suggested we just call ourselves the Daughters.

"That's not much of a name," I said.

"How about the Darling Daughters?" said Susan, and everyone laughed.

"How about the Daring Daughters?" I said.

"Hmmm, sounds mysterious," said Sheila.

"Yeah, but I like that," said Phyllis, leaning forward.

"But what would it mean?" asked Susan.

"Everyone would have to do one daring thing a day."

"A *day*?" they asked, rolling their eyes.

"Well, a week, then," I said. "And we'd have to tell what it was at each meeting."

We did get some new members for the club when we changed our name to Daring Daughters, but it turned out that doing brave things wasn't always that easy. We finally decided that "daring" could also mean something like playing a trick on someone.

"Next week will be a good time to start," said Phyllis.

"Yeah," said Donna. "On Halloween!"

During the days afterward, I started thinking about what kind of daring thing to do for a Halloween trick. Susan and I had already decided to go trick or treating together, so we'd both have to plan this together. I talked to her about it the next day on our way to school.

"I've got an idea for a daring deed," I said.

"Already?" she said. "I couldn't think of any."

I grinned. "Remember Margaret O'Brien in 'Meet Me in St. Louis'?"

"Oh, yeah," said Susan. "I saw that movie. What about it?"

"Remember how she threw flour at that man when she rang his doorbell on Halloween?"

Susan's eyebrows shot up. "We couldn't do that!"

"I could," I said.

She shook her head. "Not in someone's face!"

She was right. I probably couldn't. "But we could throw it on the floor!" I said, grinning mischievously.

I kept talking about it until Susan finally agreed. We decided to dress like tramps, just as Margaret O'Brien had done, and we'd save our daring deed for the last thing that night. We would sneak over to the other end of Valley Green, where old Mr. Putnam lived. We had never seen him, but everyone said he was a grouch, so he deserved to be tricked. His house was far back from the street, but we could run off as soon as we were finished. I thought it would be a cinch, but I was wrong.

Chapter 4

1952

During the week before Halloween, I got my tramp costume together—mostly old clothes of my dad's. My mother helped me make some rips in them, and she sewed plaid patches on the knees.

When Jeremy saw us working on the clothes, he said, "You'd better put some dirt on them if you want to look like a tramp." Later he helped me smear them with ashes from the fireplace. Brothers can come in handy sometimes.

I had thought that sneaking some flour out of the kitchen might be the hardest part of getting ready. As it turned out, though, I got my chance the next day after school. My mother was over at our next-door neighbor's, and Jeremy was listening to the radio up in his room. I slipped into the kitchen, scooped up some flour from the canister, and dumped it into a small paper bag. Then I hid the bag in my closet.

Finally, Halloween night arrived. My mother helped me get dressed because my costume had to be fastened with big safety pins. When I got everything on—dirty white shirt, ragged tweed jacket (I'd slipped the flour bag into a pocket), and large, baggy pants, Mother smiled and said, "You look like a tramp, all right!" After that she pinned up my straggly hair, and I clapped on an old floppy brown hat of Jeremy's to complete the costume. I checked myself out in my full-length mirror. *Just like Margaret O'Brien!* I thought, grinning impishly at my reflection.

My brother was still in the living room when we came downstairs. "Aren't you going to the party at church?" Mother asked him.

"Not till seven," he said. Jeremy had started junior high that fall, and he had joined our church's youth group. "Besides," he said, "I'm too big for trick or treating now."

"Who cares?" I said. "I'll be the one who gets all the candy!"

Jeremy ignored me and dipped into the fireplace ashes again. "Come here, tramp," he said, grabbing me. "You need smudges on your face." He gleefully smeared ashes on both of my cheeks until I pulled away.

"That's enough, Jeremy," said Mother.

Daddy came into the room and looked me up and down. "Great!" he said, "except for one thing. They'll know you're a girl when they see your shoes."

I looked down at my blue sneakers and frowned. Daddy was right. When I looked up, he said, "Don't worry. I'll get my old shoes from the basement. You can wear those."

"They're too big," I protested, knowing how huge my dad's feet were. I'd have to be able to run—and run fast—after we threw the flour.

"So what?" said Jeremy. "All you're going to do is walk around the neighborhood, Kath."

If only you knew, I thought. But I said, "I know, but I still could trip."

"Nonsense," called Daddy over his shoulder, "you'll

be fine." He disappeared down the basement steps and returned in a few moments waving his old brown loafers. "You can leave your own shoes on," he chuckled, "and just wear these over them."

So I agreed to wear his shoes after I had tried them on and knew I could kick them off in a hurry, if I had to.

Susan was waiting in the doorway when I slowly mounted her front steps. Walking in my dad's shoes was no easy trick.

"You look great!" she said, peeking out from under an old straw hat.

"You do too!" I said, grinning back.

Mrs. Marshall appeared in the doorway and planted a kiss on Susan's smudgy cheek. "You two make wonderful tramps," she said, laughing as we turned to go down the steps. "Have fun!"

Having fun should have been enough. If I had it to do over again, I would have taken my candy home when we finished trick or treating. We should never have rung that last doorbell. But all too soon it was time for the daring deed.

Sheila and Phyllis had been with us, and we had told them what we planned to do afterward.

"You want to go with us?" I asked.

"Not me," said Phyllis. "My mother said I have to come right home."

"Mine, too," said Sheila. "Besides, I did my deed already."

"What was it?" asked Susan.

"Tell you at the next meeting," she replied teasingly as they turned to leave.

We waved good-bye and headed for the south end of Valley Green, where the Putnam house stood. The wind had picked up, and I shuddered, wishing I had worn my coat.

"You cold?" asked Susan.

"Not much," I said.

"Think we should go home?"

"Don't be silly. We've gotta do our daring deed."

"We don't have to, you know," she said, stopping.

"We do, too!" I shot back. "You're not going to be a scaredy-cat, are you?"

Susan shook her head and fell into step beside me, but we didn't say anything to each other for a while.

Dry leaves swirled and rolled along the sidewalks, and I wondered if it might start to rain. I remembered Jeremy saying once, "If you don't like the weather in Maryland, just wait a minute!" Well, it sure changed fast that night.

The Putnam house wasn't really a part of our housing development. My dad had told us when we first moved there that the Putnams used to farm the land that Valley Green was built on. Their old wooden farmhouse, set far back from the street, was almost hidden now by overgrown bushes. Above the bushes, the second floor windows were tightly shuttered, as if to block out the sight of the little brick homes that had sprouted where their corn used to grow. Unlike those houses, though, where porch lights welcomed the trick or treaters, the Putnam house stood dark and almost unnoticed. A sagging wire fence ran along the sidewalk, and a rusty gate hung open at their front walk.

Once inside the fence, I stopped and kicked off my dad's loafers. "Better safe than sorry," I said, and Susan agreed. I left them there in the leaves so I could grab them later.

We picked our way up the uneven brick path toward the house, where a dim light barely shone from a window on the first floor. As we neared the dark porch, we noticed a car in the driveway.

"Well, at least he's home," said Susan quietly.

"Yeah," I said, "I was beginning to wonder."

"You ever seen him?" she asked.

"No, but Jeannie and Phyllis have. He's real spooky. Never talks to people—just stares at them."

"I hope he can't run fast."

"You still scared?" I asked, almost wishing she'd turn and run, so I could, too.

"Not really," she said.

Suddenly, we heard a loud bang. "What's that?" I said, grabbing Susan. There was another bang—and another. We listened, terrified. The banging continued, and then we could tell it was coming from alongside the house.

Suddenly Susan giggled. "It's just a shutter!" she whispered. Sure enough, by straining I could see an upstairs shutter hanging by one hinge. Each gust of wind made it bang against the house.

Feeling braver, we silently climbed the creaky porch steps. With knowing nods, we each reached into our jacket pockets and grabbed a fistful of flour. I felt around on the door frame until I found the bell. Then I pushed it hard.

Chapter 5

1952

We stood in the darkness and waited a few minutes before I rang the bell again. Suddenly, an overhead light flooded the porch, and the door flew open. We tossed our flour and bolted down the steps. I remember seeing a startled man with flour on his legs and shoes. I heard him yell, and a woman saying, "I'll get 'em!"

As I ran, I glanced back and saw her chasing us. We were far ahead and would have made it safely out of the yard if I hadn't gone and tripped. I went sprawling, and a sharp pain shot into my knee.

Susan stopped beside me. I sat up and grabbed at my knee, fighting back tears.

"Whadya guys think you're doing!" yelled the woman, who had caught up with us. She yanked at my arm.

I struggled to my feet, and as I did, my hat fell off. She let go of my arm. "Why," she said, "you're a girl!"

I nodded, wiping my face with my sleeve. "Sorry," I mumbled. "We didn't mean anything." I was trembling all over. I glanced at Susan. She looked like she might faint.

"Sorry, you say?" said the woman disgustedly.

"What kinda kids are you, anyway?"

"It was just a Halloween trick," I said.

The woman clapped her hands on her hips. "Some kinda trick, throwing flour at a poor old man! And he was gonna give you some candy."

"I'm sorry," I said, shaking my head.

And Susan added quietly, "We really are."

"You get outta here before I call the cops!"

I tried to say more, but the woman spun around and headed back to the house. We hustled out of the yard and up the street, never stopping until, out of breath, we reached Susan's house. By that time I was limping badly.

Under the streetlight, I knelt and inspected my knee. Blood had soaked into my pants leg and down onto my sock. And my knee really hurt. "You want to come in?" Susan asked. "My mother can fix you up."

I shook my head. "I'd better get home." Suddenly, though, I gave Susan a big hug. "Thanks for sticking by me," I said.

She looked surprised. "I wouldn't have left you there alone, Kathy," she said.

I smiled. "Someone else might have."

"Not me! Not your best friend!"

"My forever friend!" I corrected, and I hugged her again.

As I turned to leave, Susan said, "What are you gonna tell your parents?"

I shrugged. "Nothing. Just that I fell, I guess."

It wasn't that simple, though. They knew right away we'd been up to something besides just going door to door. As my mother was dabbing at my scraped knee with a soapy washcloth, she said, "My goodness, honey, you must have fallen awfully hard."

I sniffed, "I was hurrying."

"What was the rush?"

"It was getting late."

She started asking questions, but Daddy interrupted. "It's Halloween, Marge. Kids can have a few secrets!"

I sighed with relief, thinking that was the end of it, but then my dad said, "Are my shoes on the porch?"

"Your shoes?" I had forgotten all about them. My mind raced for an answer. "Um—I took them off. It was hard to walk in them."

"But where are they?"

"They're—they're down the street."

"What?"

I looked up at him and said quietly, "They're at the Putnams'."

His raised his eyebrows. "What were you doing way down there?"

"Ringing doorbells." Well, I told myself, that much was true.

It was past my bedtime by then, and we had school the next day, so Daddy drove me down to get the shoes. They were right on the lawn where I'd left them, and no one was in sight.

My parents never did ask any more about it, but I felt guilty every time I thought about Mr. Putnam after that. Of course, I still planned to brag about it at the next meeting of the Daring Daughters.

Just about everyone who showed up the following Monday had Halloween tricks to tell about. We giggled while Sheila told how she and some kids had wrapped a roll of toilet paper around someone's bush. Donna and her brother had knocked over a garbage can.

"Mine's better than that!" said Nancy. "I threw a raw egg at the Kendalls' front door!"

"You didn't!" said Phyllis. Suddenly everyone was quiet.

Nancy nodded, but she looked a little sheepish.

I cleared my throat. "Well," I said, "you've got to admit that was a daring deed, all right." Everyone agreed, but no one laughed anymore.

Before Nancy's story, I'd thought everyone would love to hear what Susan and I had done. We'd decided ahead of time to save our adventure until everyone else had finished telling theirs. Somehow, though, our story fell flat.

"That sounds like what Margaret O'Brien did once in a movie," said Donna.

"It was," I announced, "only scarier!" But now I didn't really think so.

No one said much after that about doing any more daring deeds. Susan had been pretty quiet at the meeting, and she and I never mentioned Mr. Putnam again.

So that was the end of the Daring Daughters. Rehearsals were starting after school for the Christmas program, and I think everyone was glad for an excuse not to make the meetings anymore. Even me and Susan.

Chapter 6

1952

The upper grades at Valley Green Elementary gave a Christmas concert every year for the PTA. I had sung in it in 1949, when I was in the fifth grade, and I did again in 1950. Our new music teacher that year, Miss Phillips, said she wanted to have a few special numbers for the concert, and some of the kids in our sixth-grade class said Susan and I should sing a duet. They'd heard us at school, and some of them had heard us sing at some special church programs, too.

"Do you want to try it?" asked Miss Phillips. Since she was new to Valley Green, she didn't know any of us very well yet. My mother had said she was "fresh out of college."

I thought it would be fun for the two of us to sing together, but Susan wasn't so sure. "I think I'd be too nervous to get up in front of the whole school like that," she said, "and all the parents, too."

"Don't be silly!" I said. "It's no different from singing in church. There's nothing to it."

"Maybe you don't think it is, but I know me. I'd be scared stiff."

I kept coaxing and coaxing until finally Susan agreed to do it. Miss Phillips was pleased, and the next day she said, "How would you girls like to try 'White Christmas' for the program? That's fun to harmonize, and I'm sure you'd sing it well." She asked us to stay after class so we could run through it.

Our music teacher was right. "White Christmas" was easy, and I was more eager than ever to sing the duet. I could imagine the two of us onstage in the assembly hall, with all the kids and our parents smiling at us as we sang. I could almost hear the applause we'd get when we were finished.

Susan, though, still wasn't sure about singing before so many people. "What if I forget the words?" she said. "I'd die of embarrassment!"

"Just learn it well," said Miss Phillips. "You've got three whole weeks." And before we left that day, she gave us a copy of the music to practice at home so that we'd know it by heart. "It would be good," she said, "if you could memorize the verse as well as the chorus."

I had read the verse. It was about being in California at Christmas time, where the grass was green and the sun was shining. "That's the way it was when we lived there," I said, nodding, "but my family still had Christmas."

"Of course you did," said Miss Phillips, "but the songwriter was living far away from his home, where it always snowed at that time of year, and the verse explains that he was homesick."

As we walked home, Susan said to me, "Do you want to keep the music at your house? You've got the hardest part."

I tossed my head. "Not really. I know most of it already. All I have to learn is the verse, and that's easy."

She nodded. "Well, next time you come over, I'll get my mother to play the whole thing for us."

Mrs. Marshall did play it for us the very next day. After we sang it all the way through, she went over the alto part a couple of extra times to help me learn the harmony.

One day as I was leaving Susan's house, her mother said, "I am so pleased, Kathy, that you got Susan to try the duet. She's always been rather shy about singing in front of large groups."

"That's okay," I said, and then I punched Susan playfully. "I'll hold her up if she starts to faint." And we all laughed.

One day the following week, when I came home from school, my mother had just arrived home from a shopping trip in Washington. "Guess what!" she said. "I met Mildred Marshall when I stopped for lunch today." She hung her coat in the living room closet and continued, "While we were eating, we decided you girls should have something special for singing in the Christmas program."

My eyes lit up. "Something special?"

"To wear when you sing." She handed me a store bag. "I hope it fits," she said.

I reached in eagerly, and a red taffeta dress unfolded in my hands. It had a lace collar and long sleeves and a wide velvet sash. "It's beautiful!" I said.

Mother beamed. "Mildred bought a green one just like it for Susan."

I tried it on right away and stood admiring myself in the tall mirror on mother's closet door. The wide skirt flared out as I twirled around. It was longer than any I had ever worn. "It's wonderful!" I said, giving my mother a hug. "Thank you so much!"

"I'll shorten the skirt, of course," she said.

"Oh no! This is just right," I said, twirling again.

"But none of your other skirts . . ."

"I want it this way," I said, pouting. "All the girls are wearing longer skirts now."

Mother just shrugged. She had learned not to argue with me once I made up my mind about clothes.

I began marking the days off on the calendar, and the big night was just about all I talked about at home. I was sure that Susan and I would be the hit of the program. Jeremy was the first one who got sick of hearing about it. "I'll be glad when that concert's over!" he said one day.

"You're just jealous," I snapped back. "You didn't mind all the fuss when you got your Life Award!"

"That was different. I *earned* that!"

"Well, I earned this, too," I said. But inside I knew I really hadn't worked very hard at it, and not nearly as long as Jeremy had worked as a Boy Scout to earn that rank.

Finally, the day of the big night arrived. Miss Phillips had us rehearsing in the assembly hall most of the afternoon. Three long wooden steps—she called them "risers"—were set up on the floor in front of the stage for the chorus to stand on. The boys were in the back, on the highest riser, the altos on the middle one, and the sopranos stood on the lowest riser and along the floor in front of us.

Before we started to rehearse, the kids in the band sat up on the stage, each practicing what sounded like a different song as they tooted on their horns or struggled with their violins. Some of the boys in the chorus held their hands over their ears.

Down on the floor, facing all of us, Miss Phillips stood at the piano. She always played standing up, either bobbing her head to direct our singing or playing with one hand and waving the other.

She went through the whole program to make sure we all knew what to do and when to do it. We liked the songs she had chosen for us, especially one that had come out a year earlier, called "Rudolph, the Red-Nosed Reindeer." Most of us knew the words because we heard it played all the time on the radio.

"Now, after you finish singing 'Rudolph,'" said Miss Phillips, "Susan and Kathy will come forward for the last number on the program—'White Christmas.'"

The best one of all, I thought. Susan looked back at me, and we winked at each other.

The teacher looked at us and continued, "You two slip over to the piano as quickly as possible—right here. Then, after you finish singing, everyone—all of you and the whole audience—will sing it through again."

"Kathy," said Miss Phillips, motioning, "you'd better stand at the end of that riser so you won't have to climb over anyone when it's time for the duet."

I moved past Jeannie Grayson and the Moberg twins, and I smiled down at our teacher when I reached my new place at the edge of the riser. Miss Phillips waited until everyone got quiet, and then she motioned for the two of us to come forward. I stepped down to the floor and over to the piano, where Susan stood waiting. When we finished "White Christmas," Miss Phillips beamed. "You'll do great!" she said. I couldn't wait for that night.

Chapter 1

1952

Mother fixed my dinner early because I had to be at school by 6:30. I had just taken a bath, so I ate in my blue chenille robe. "Wait till you see the stage, Mother," I said, chewing as I talked. "It's all decorated with evergreens and big red flowers in pots."

"Poinsettias?" she asked.

"I don't know, but they're beautiful!" I pushed back my plate. "I can't eat any more. Can I get dressed now?"

Mother laughed and shooed me out of the kitchen. Jeremy just rolled his eyes.

My father drove Susan and me to the school because it was dark by then, and windy. We sat next to him on the broad front seat, snuggled down in our wool coats and glad for the warmth of the car. Neither of us had ever been driven to school before, and certainly never at night.

"Well," said Daddy, turning onto Oak Street, where the school was, "I hope everything goes well tonight."

"Don't worry," I said, "we'll be fine." I looked over at Susan, but she didn't say anything.

As we pulled up at the entrance, Daddy gave me a quick peck on the cheek. "Here you go," he said. "Two

Cinderellas arriving at the ball."

I giggled and followed Susan out into the cold air. "Hope the coach doesn't turn into a pumpkin!" I called to my dad as I shut the car door.

The cafeteria, where we had been told to meet, was buzzing when we came in. The boys, looking almost like strangers in their white shirts and ties, stood around joking or jostling with each other at one side of the room. The girls chattered among themselves, raving about each others' dresses.

Susan and I dumped our coats onto the pile on one of the tables. Her green dress looked wonderful on her, and I wondered, with a flickering of jealousy, whether everyone would be looking at her instead of both of us when we sang.

Jeannie Grayson came in just then, breathless, with rosy cheeks and a nose to match. "Guess what!" she said, unbuttoning her coat. "Freddie Baker's here."

"Beverly's little brother?" said Susan.

"Yeah," said Jeannie, "I just saw him in the hall."

I knitted my brow. "Isn't he the one who's crippled?"

Jeannie nodded, adding her coat to the pile. "His father lifted Freddie's wheelchair in through the door, but he can move it along all by himself."

"What happened to him?" I asked.

"Beverly told me," said Susan, "that he caught polio one summer when his family lived in Texas."

"Boy," I said, "I'm glad we never had to live there."

"You can catch polio anywhere," said Susan. "My father said so."

"Sure," said Jeannie. "President Roosevelt caught it in Canada."

I nodded, remembering pictures of our last president

sitting in his wheelchair or leaning on a cane.

Miss Phillips came bouncing into the room. She had on a red silky dress and high heels. Her long blond hair was turned under on the ends, and it swished as she moved around. I thought she was beautiful, even though my mother had said she didn't look like a teacher.

In a few minutes Miss Phillips had us all lined up, just the way we had practiced that afternoon. "Now remember," she said, "be dignified. Go in quietly, and don't wave at anybody when you get up on the risers!"

As we filed into the assembly hall, I caught my breath. I'd never seen so many people in there before—mothers and fathers and grandparents, and lots of children, too. Extra chairs had been set up in the aisles, and some little kids were even sitting on the floor near the piano.

When I reached my place on the risers, my eyes swept the audience until I found my parents and Jeremy about halfway back. The Marshalls sat next to them, and right down in front was our junior choir director from church, Mrs. Fritz. She must have known that half of her choir was in this concert. I wanted to wave at all of them, but I remembered not to.

I glanced at Susan down in the front row. If she was scared, she didn't look it. She just stood there calmly, watching the teacher like everybody else. When Miss Phillips raised her arms to direct the first song, I smiled. This was going to be a perfect evening.

The first half of the program went just as we had rehearsed. Sometimes the chorus sang, sometimes the band played, and sometimes we sang with the band. Kenny Goodwin played "The March of the Toy Soldiers" on his clarinet, and Phyllis Morrison sang "Silent Night." She was flat on some of the notes, but everyone applauded politely when she was finished. *Never mind,* I thought, *Susan and I will make up for it.*

It was while we were singing "Rudolph, the Red-Nosed Reindeer" that the trouble started. I knew Susan and I were singing next, and just the thought of it made my stomach tighten. Then a terrible thing happened: all the little kids sitting down in front started singing "Rudolph" with us. Pretty soon everyone was singing—all the parents and everyone in the audience. *No,* I thought, *not yet!* They're not supposed to sing until after Susan and I sing "White Christmas." I could feel my heart pounding. This isn't the way we planned it. They were singing the wrong song!

When "Rudolph" ended, I thought they'd never stop clapping. Finally, the audience was quiet again, and Miss Phillips motioned to Susan and me. But as I went to step down from the risers, my heel caught in the hem of my long skirt. I tripped and fell down on the floor, landing hard. Miss Phillips and some other grownups rushed over as I scrambled to my feet.

"Are you okay?" they asked.

I nodded and followed my teacher over to the piano, fighting back tears. Susan took my hand and squeezed it as Miss Phillips played the opening bars of "White Christmas." I could feel my legs shaking, and my hands shook, too. All too soon it was time to sing. Susan sang right out, as if she'd been singing to crowds all her life. But when I opened my mouth, I couldn't remember a single word!

Miss Phillips' eyebrows shot up. But Susan—my wonderful, best friend—kept right on going. She sang the entire verse by herself, every word just exactly right, every note just perfect. As I listened, I began to remember, too, but I didn't even try to join her at that point. I waited until my knees quieted down and I was sure I'd found my voice again. When it was time for the chorus, Susan and I glanced at each other, smiled, and harmonized just the way we had planned.

While the audience applauded, I hugged Susan. I could feel tears rolling down my cheeks, but I couldn't stop them. Then Miss Phillips turned and gestured for the people to join in, and everyone sang the chorus again, all the way to the end. Some kids were still singing it as we left the assembly hall.

When we got back to the lunch room, I said to Susan, "How did you do it? You sang the whole verse by yourself!"

Susan smiled as she slipped into her coat. "I did what Mrs. Fritz told us last week. Don't you remember what she said to do about stage fright? 'Just forget yourself, and think only about the music.'"

I'm sure I blushed when she said that. And no wonder. The only thing I had been thinking about that night was myself! *Next time,* I thought, *I'll listen carefully to Mrs. Fritz.*

As we walked to the car, my parents told me they'd never been so proud of me. Even Jeremy said the music was good. *And my coach didn't turn into a pumpkin,* I thought, as I climbed back into our car. But on the ride home I made Mother promise she'd shorten my skirt three inches before I ever wore that red dress again.

Chapter 6

1952

On Memorial Day of 1951, the year I finished sixth grade, a long-awaited swimming pool opened in Valley Green. My parents quickly bought a family membership, and so did the Marshalls and a lot of my other friends' parents. To celebrate the opening, the neighborhood association had planned a picnic on the grounds next to the pool. Most fathers, of course, had the day off, so whole families were attending, including ours. Mr. and Mrs. Marshall had to go to a wedding in Philadelphia that same day, so Susan came with us to the picnic.

When the five of us arrived at 11:00 that morning, charcoal smoke was already swirling above the grills. We lugged our picnic supplies and chairs across the field and claimed one of the new wooden tables that sat under the trees near the pool. Daddy and I unfolded the lawn chairs while Mother unpacked the picnic basket. "The weather couldn't be better," she said, smiling, as she spread a red-and-white checked cloth over the table.

Jeremy looked up, shading his eyes against the sun. "Not a cloud anywhere," he said, and a few moments later he asked, "Can we eat right away? I'm starved."

"You're always hungry these days," laughed Mother, lifting paper plates from the basket.

"I want to eat too," I said, rubbing my palms together, "so we can get into that pool." Susan and I had worn our suits so we wouldn't have to waste any time later.

"Not until an hour after lunch," cautioned Daddy.

I pouted. "You always say that," I said, trying to sound as disgusted as possible.

Jeremy said, "You don't want to get stomach cramps in the water, do you?"

I tossed my head. "I don't see what's so dangerous about cramps. I'd just get out of the pool if I got any."

"You might not be able to, dummy," he said. "You could double over and drown."

I looked at Susan and rolled my eyes.

"That's okay," she said. "My parents won't let me go in right after lunch either."

Mother placed packages of hot dog and hamburger rolls alongside some plastic containers she had unpacked. She gave Daddy some thawing hamburger patties and hot dogs in a plastic bag. "Here," she said, "the sooner these start cooking, the sooner we can eat. And girls," she added, handing us the long barbecue fork and tongs, "you can carry these."

We were watching the meat sizzling on the grill when Jeannie Grayson came running up. "You haven't eaten yet?" she asked.

We shook our heads.

"Well, come on over as soon as you can," she said. "They're opening the pool at noon." Then she lowered her voice. "Kenny Goodwin's here."

"I know," I said quietly. "I already saw him." I always noticed when Kenny was around.

Sheila Wilkins came by a few minutes later. "I think our whole class is here today!" she said.

Susan smiled and said, "This summer's going to be great!"

Sheila smoothed her hair back and looked around. "Did Jeremy come?" she asked. I knew she had a crush on my brother.

"I think he's down pitching horseshoes," I said. We could hear the clanging from far across the field as iron shoes struck the metal stake. "He said he wanted to get in a quick game before we ate—and before it gets too crowded. This place is filling up fast." By then all the tables were taken. Families were spreading blankets on the grass to set their picnic things on.

"Well, see you at the pool," said Sheila, running off.

By noon we'd finished eating, but, of course, it was too soon to go in swimming.

"Can't we just go and watch?" I begged my parents, bouncing up and down. I knew Susan was just as eager as I was, but she was probably trying to be polite.

And even Jeremy said, "We won't swim yet, we promise."

Finally, Daddy gave in and said he'd go over to the pool with us. "But remember," he said, as we hurried along, "no going in the water. One o'clock will be here before you know it, and then you can swim all you want."

I wished later that I hadn't begged the way I did. At the time, though, it had seemed so important not to miss a moment of that opening day.

Jeremy headed for a group of his friends as soon as we came to the pool area. Daddy settled down in a deck chair, and Susan and I stood around watching the kids jostling and splashing. I wondered if there would even be room for us by the time one o'clock came.

We heard someone calling. "Hey, Kathy! Susan!" It was Kenny Goodwin. We waved, and he said, "Come on in!"

"Can't yet," we called back. "Not till one." I pointed to where my watch usually was on my wrist.

Kenny nodded and swam away.

Fifteen minutes dragged by, and finally, at 12:45, Daddy said we could go in as long as we stayed together and didn't try swimming.

"Yippee!" I said, as we scampered off and jumped in.

The water was colder than I expected, but soon I forgot that as Susan and I bobbed over to where Kenny stood with a bunch of other boys. They were all watching the same spot in the water and counting, "Twenty-one, twenty-two, twenty-three . . ."

Jerry Wilson sprang up from under the water, his hair plastered to his head and water streaming down his face. He took a big gulping breath and rubbed his eyes with both hands.

"You win so far," someone shouted.

"What's going on?" I asked, grinning.

"Contest," said Jerry, panting.

"To see who can stay under longest," said Kenny. "You wanna try?"

Susan and I looked at each other. "Sure," we said, and I added, "Long as we don't have to swim." I glanced over to where my father was sitting, but he was busy talking to somebody.

We didn't do too well the first time we tried it, but the boys said we'd get another turn later. The contest was simple. Two people held their noses and ducked under together while the others counted. Chip Grayson was the champ so far, out of seven boys. He'd stayed under until thirty-nine.

By the time it was our turn again, Jeannie and Sheila had joined us. Just then, though, someone tossed a small red ball into the water. The boys darted over to it and started tossing it back and forth, forgetting the breath-holding contest.

"Nuts!" said Susan, pouting.

I wasn't going to let that stop us. "Let's just have a girls' contest," I said.

"Yeah," said Sheila, "All duck under at the same time, and the last one up wins!" We all grabbed our noses and disappeared under the water.

I've never been good at holding my breath long, but when I finally jumped up, Jeannie and Sheila were already waiting. Susan, though, was nowhere in sight. "Susan wins!" they yelled, but just then some boys came by, and the girls took off after them.

I looked around for Susan. So many kids were splashing that it was hard to see who was nearby, and my eyes stung from the chlorine. I kept turning around, certain that she'd pop up any second, but she didn't. I panicked. *No! Don't tell me she got stomach cramps! She must be doubled over under the water somewhere!* "Help!" I screamed. "Help! My friend's drowning!"

Chapter

1952

My eyes swept the crowded water. I couldn't see Susan anywhere. "She's gone!" I cried, my hands clapped to my face.

"What's the matter?" someone said.

"My friend! I can't find her!"

I started to shout for the lifeguard, but someone else grabbed my arm. "Kathy!"

I spun around. It was Susan! "Oh, thank goodness!" I said, hugging her hard. Then I dropped my hands, and my eyes narrowed. "Where were you, anyway?"

"I swallowed some water as we went under, and I started coughing."

"But where did you go? We thought you were still down holding your breath."

"I came up over there." She gestured with her head. "I waited and watched for you, but there were too many people in the way. Finally I came back over." She put an arm around me. "Sorry if I scared you."

I shrugged and swung at her playfully. "And here I thought you were doubled over or something." *And if I hadn't begged to go in the water early,* I thought,

I wouldn't have had that to worry about.

And so Memorial Day ended happily—the first day of two full months of fun at the pool.

Starting in June, the Red Cross offered swimming lessons, and everyone signed up. Jeremy was working on his lifesaving badge by then, so he enrolled in the classes, too. He and Susan and I rode over on our bikes in the morning, came home for lunch, and then went back again later. When Jeremy didn't go, my mother or Mrs. Marshall stayed with us. On those days, though, we never went until afternoon. "I'll be glad when Susan and I can go by ourselves," I grumbled once. "It's no fun having to waste a whole morning!"

"Well," said Mother, "whenever you want to do the laundry and scrub the kitchen floor for me, just let me know."

That kept me quiet, especially since I knew that next year we'd be able to go without our mothers.

By late July of that first year, word began to spread that Valley Green pool might be a dangerous place to be. "What do you mean, dangerous?" I asked Sheila when she told me about it.

"People are catching polio in swimming pools," she said.

"Ah, go on," I said.

"It's true. My father said so."

The fear of polio itself was nothing new to anyone. Every summer for years, thousands of people—especially children—died or became lame after catching the disease. No one knew for sure how it spread, but everyone was afraid of crowds in the summertime. By August of each year, our parents wouldn't let us go to the movies, and my dad and Jeremy even stopped going to baseball games. And with so many new pools in the Washington area, more and more people seemed to have come down with it after swimming.

Our own Valley Green pool closed the first week in August. I suppose my parents were relieved, considering the risks, but I fussed about it for days. "No one around here ever caught polio," I said. "Why pick on us?"

"No one's picking on you, Kathy," said my father. "It's just plain common sense not to go where you could catch anything as serious as polio." And that settled it.

The following summer—in 1952—everyone hoped there wouldn't be another epidemic. Susan and I had turned twelve and had almost finished seventh grade when the pool opened that year. And it was then that our parents started letting us go there by ourselves. They knew we'd both become good swimmers, and a lifeguard was always on duty.

"Guess what!" said Susan one day early in July. "Kenny says he's taking diving lessons this year."

"He is?" I said. "Let's sign up!" The thought of being in the same diving class with Kenny Goodwin just about made me swoon.

Susan shook her head. "Don't get excited. He told me the classes are filled until August, so none of us can take any until then."

"I can wait," I said, and told myself it would be worth it to be in the same class with Kenny.

By the middle of July, though, Jeremy said, "Looks like they're going to close the pool early again this year."

I stiffened. "Why?"

"Same as last year. Polio."

"There's no polio around here."

"Shows how much you know, Kathy," said Jeremy, tossing his head. "Don't you listen to the news? In the

Washington area—that's us, you know—reported cases are at an all-time high."

I flipped back my hair. "Well, I don't know anyone who's caught it."

"That's smart, Kathy. Just pretend it isn't happening."

"I didn't say that it isn't—I just . . . Oh, never mind!" I marched up to my room and shut the door. *Jeremy always thinks he knows everything,* I thought.

But it turned out that Jeremy was right. The next day we heard on the radio that the polio rate was already becoming the highest in history. All area swimming pools were going to close the following weekend.

That evening, after most of the TV news had been about the polio epidemic, Daddy turned off the set and said, "That's it for this year." He started to leave the living room.

I spun around. "What do you mean?"

"No more using the pool."

"They haven't closed it yet."

"You just heard what they said, Kathy."

"But, Daddy . . ." I wailed.

Mother interrupted. "You heard your father. Swimming pools are dangerous places right now."

I crossed my arms. "Nobody knows what causes polio!"

Jeremy stood up. "There's definitely a connection between polio and swimming in public pools," he said. "I don't like it either, Kathy, but you have to use your head."

"Oh, shut up, Jeremy!" I said.

"Watch your tongue, young lady," said Daddy. "And we'll have no back talk about this, either. No more swimming this year!"

Chapter 10

1952

On Friday, July 18th—I'll never forget that date as long as I live—Daddy was at work, and Jeremy and a friend had taken the bus into Washington for the day. I was eating a late breakfast when my mother reminded me that she had to help out at the church rummage sale that day. I frowned as I poured milk on my cereal. She was always going somewhere. First it was PTA, then a bridge club, and now this church committee.

"Do you want to go with me, Kathy?" asked Mother, wiping off the toaster. "They can always use an extra pair of hands."

I looked over at her. "Is the place going to be full of smelly old clothes like last year?"

Mother smiled. "That's what rummage is, Kathy— old things people don't want anymore." She started wiping off the counter. "There are always people who'll buy them, though. We may make more money this year than . . ."

"I think I'll skip it this time," I said.

"Well, if you don't go, you can at least clean up your room. It looks like a cyclone struck it."

"It's too hot upstairs, and besides, I don't mind the mess."

"Well, I do, and I refuse to clean it when there's stuff all over the place."

"Never mind, I'll do it," I replied.

"Today."

I shrugged my shoulders and continued eating. Here it was, only mid-July, I thought, and what were we kids supposed to do for the rest of the summer without the pool? We should have been able to go one last time. Susan's parents probably wouldn't let her go anymore either, of course. But it just wasn't fair!

Mother had said as she left for the church that Susan could come for lunch, so I called her and she came over on her bike. We carried our sandwiches and lemonade outside and sat at the picnic table under the maple tree. Susan had pulled her hair back into a long ponytail. As we sat down, I wished for the hundredth time that I had dark, wavy hair like hers, instead of dishwater blond.

After I finished my sandwich, I took a final sip of lemonade and sat cradling the empty glass in my hand. "Today may be the hottest on record," I said.

Susan nodded. "I know. You're lucky your dad bought that air conditioner."

"Yeah, but it only cools off the living room."

"So what? That's better than having the whole house hot like ours is."

I had to agree. Daddy said he'd put the air conditioner in the living room so that we could be cool while we watched TV, but I think he also wanted the neighbors to see it in the window.

My dad liked to be the first on the block to get things for the house. We had the first TV and the first chain link fence, and pretty soon everyone else on Lotus Lane had them, too. Now he was adding a screened porch, and he was always working on it whenever he was at home.

I looked over at Susan. "What do you want to do?" I said. "It's too hot to ride very far on our bikes."

She waited a little and said, "Maybe we could watch TV." Our screen was much larger than the Marshalls', so Susan always liked to watch at my house. But then she added, "There's nothing on now, though."

I agreed. I set down my glass firmly and said, "I've been thinking."

Susan looked over at me.

"About the pool," I continued.

"We can't go *there*, Kathy."

I frowned. "I don't think it's fair that we can't go just one last time."

"Maybe not, but you know what our parents said."

I leaned forward. "Look, there hasn't been a single case of polio in Valley Green."

"So?"

"So our pool's okay. It just figures."

Susan sighed and was quiet for a few moments. Then she looked up and said slowly, "You mean, you want to go swimming *anyway*?"

I shrugged. "We could, you know. The pool's still open."

Susan shook her head. "But our parents . . ."

"I don't think they understand. Our pool is safe." I lifted my hair from my sweaty neck. "They're just overprotective. And besides, nobody knows what causes polio—you know that."

I could usually be pretty convincing with Susan. It worked that day too. After we cleaned up the kitchen, she went home to get her things, and shortly after one o'clock we met at the pool entrance.

"Mother was sewing downstairs," said Susan, squinting at me in the sunlight. "She didn't even notice me."

I grinned at her. "Good work," I said, and then I added, giggling, "One last daring deed, Susan!" I remember, though, that she didn't say anything.

We wheeled our bikes over to the rack, locked them in place, and headed for the bathhouse.

Chapter 11

1952

We changed in a hurry. Susan had a brand new bathing suit, a bright blue-green one. She called it "turquoise."

"Wow!" I said, "It has a built-in bra!"

Susan smiled. "Just a little one," she said, checking herself out in one of the mirrors. "You might need one soon yourself."

"I doubt it," I said. "I'll probably be flat-chested forever."

"Silly girl!" said Susan, swishing her towel at me.

As we headed for the water, I smelled the chlorine and felt the burning sun on my bare shoulders. I was glad I'd brought suntan lotion, even though we both had pretty good tans by then.

"Not many people here," said Susan, looking around.

I shrugged. "Guess they think it'll rain." A dark cloud hovered over the baseball field.

We paused at the pool's edge, and she leaned closer. "See Kenny anywhere?"

I had already looked for him. I shook my head.

Susan smiled. "He might be around later."

"So might David," I said. I knew she liked him.

She tossed her head. "I don't care whether he comes or not." She splashed down into the water.

"Yeah, sure," I yelled, following her. "You can't fool me!"

We swam the length of the pool and back twice, and then we floated, side by side, face up. I closed my eyes to the sun, and the world turned orange. I lay there for a while, enjoying the sun's burning heat and the wonderfully cool water that lapped gently around my body.

We waited around and swam some more, but somehow it just wasn't the same that day. There were a couple of kids there we didn't know, but none of our friends showed up. Not Kenny, not David, not anyone. We left after about an hour and went back to my house.

"What'll we do with our wet suits?" asked Susan, after we had changed. "We can't hang them on the clothes line or Mrs. Cobb will tell your parents!"

Susan was right. Mrs. Cobb, our next-door neighbor, knew everybody's business and made sure everyone else heard about it as soon as possible.

"We could put them in my closet," I said.

"Yeah, but they'll take forever to dry in there."

I scratched my head. Suddenly I had an idea. "My hair dryer!"

So that's what we did. We had used my new dryer on our hair, of course, so then we tried to dry our wet suits and towels as well. After a while, though, they were still pretty damp, so I draped everything on hooks in my closet while Susan called her mother and got permission to stay until five o'clock.

We were playing Monopoly in the living room when

Mother burst in shortly after four. "Whew," she said. "I'm exhausted! We had more customers today than I've ever seen at a rummage sale." She disappeared into the kitchen, but moments later she returned with her car keys still in her hand. "Kathy," she said, "I forgot to take along that bag of outgrown clothes in your closet. I told them I'd run it over now because they might still be able to sell them." She started for the stairs.

I jumped up. "I'll get it!"

Mother paused, surprised, but I had already dashed past her. "It's okay," I said, over my shoulder. "I'll save you the trip." I ran up two steps at a time and was back in a few moments with the bag of clothes.

Mother thanked me and took it, but then she frowned and added, "I suppose you didn't clean your room, then."

I rolled my eyes. "Too hot up there," I said. I smiled sweetly. "I'll do it tomorrow morning, I promise."

After she left, Susan and I both sighed. "Close call," I said, grinning.

"Yeah, if she'd seen our suits . . ." said Susan, rolling the dice again. She'd just put a hotel on Boardwalk, so we knew the game was almost over. When she finished her turn, she said, "How will I get my stuff back?"

"I'll sneak them into my suitcase when I stay at your house next weekend," I said.

Only it never happened. The following Tuesday, July 22nd, Susan and I were supposed to meet some kids at church to plan a car wash, but she couldn't go because she was sick in bed. The next two days she was still sick. Finally, on Friday, Mrs. Marshall let her talk to me for a few minutes on the phone.

"Feeling any better?" I asked, twisting the cord around my

finger. I was hoping she would sound like her old self.

Susan's voice was so soft I had a hard time hearing her. "Not really," she said.

"Still have a fever?"

"Yeah, and I ache all over."

"Gee, that's too bad." I waited a little, but Susan didn't say anything more, so I said, "Guess I won't be staying at your house tomorrow night, huh?"

There was a pause. "Maybe next week, okay?"

"Sure," I said. I thought about her suit and towel, still hidden in my closet, and told her I'd leave them there for now.

"I won't need them," she said. I didn't know it then, of course, but that was the last thing Susan ever said to me.

When I came down for breakfast on Saturday morning, Mother was in the hallway next to the kitchen, talking on the phone. Jeremy motioned that it was Mrs. Cobb. We both hung around, wondering what story that woman was spreading this time.

My mother listened for a while, and then I heard her say, "She's been in one since early this morning?"

Who was "in" what? I wondered idly, as I padded over to the counter to pour my orange juice.

Mother stood frowning in the kitchen doorway as she listened to Mrs. Cobb. I put the lid on the juice container and set it back in the refrigerator. When I turned around, my mother looked pale. "That's the worst kind, isn't it?" she said, knitting her brow. She kept shaking her head, and finally she said, "I knew she was quite sick, but . . ."

Susan, I thought. *She's talking about Susan!* I motioned to her that I wanted to say something.

Mother put a finger to her lips. "Where could she have caught it?" she continued. "No one's using the pool anymore, so it couldn't have been that."

When I heard "pool," I froze.

Mother turned back into the hallway, but then I heard her tell Mrs. Cobb that she needed to go. She hung up and came into the kitchen.

I looked up at her, my lip trembling. "It's Susan, isn't it!" I said.

She nodded. "She's in the hospital."

"The hospital!"

"She has polio."

My stomach knotted. "No!" I said, trying to block out what I was hearing.

"She's in an iron lung. It's helping her breathe."

As if I didn't know what an iron lung was! There were pictures in the paper all the time of polio patients lying inside those big metal things with only their heads sticking out. You could see their faces in the mirrors above them. A machine squeezed their chests and made them breathe. I got scared just looking at them.

I shook my head. "Iron lungs are only for the worst cases!" I said, looking at Mother for some kind of reassurance, but she had none to give.

Instead, she put her arms around me and said quietly, "Mrs. Cobb said Susan is very, very sick, Kathy. She has bulbar polio. That's . . ."

She didn't have to tell me. I closed my eyes and pulled away, trying to close out the word "bulbar." I'd looked it up when we did a unit on polio last year in social studies. "Bulbar poliomyelitis," the encyclopedia had said, "attacks the part of the brain that controls breathing and other vital functions, and it could lead to paralysis and sometimes even . . ." I didn't want to think about the rest of it. I couldn't connect what my mother had just said with the

Susan I knew, who bounced along next to me on her bike or giggled with me in the movies. It had to be a mistake. Anything else was unthinkable.

We called the hospital and were told that Susan's condition was "very serious." She couldn't have visitors, of course, for fear they would catch polio, and even the Marshalls hardly got a chance to see their own daughter.

Whenever I saw any of my friends, they always talked about Susan, and everyone had stories about polio. Jeannie Grayson said some kid over on the other side of Valley Green had it, and her sister Carolyn said that Bobby Manley's cousin had died from it. I didn't say anything.

On Sunday, our whole church prayed for Susan. And I added a secret prayer that no one would find out about our going to the pool that day. Not ever.

Chapter 12

1952

"What does 'critical' mean?" I asked my mother after I called the hospital on Monday.

Mother had been heading for the basement with the laundry basket. She paused at the top of the steps. "Is that Susan's condition?" she asked.

I nodded.

She hesitated a moment, set the basket down, and said quietly, "That means it could go either way."

"Either way?"

"Either Susan gets through this, or . . ."

My eyes filled up. "She's not going to *die*, Mother!"

My mother hugged me silently for a few moments. Then she stood back, held my shoulders, and looked into my eyes. "Susan's getting the best of care, Kathy," was all she could say. "She's in God's hands now."

I bit my lip and nodded. The Marshalls were at the hospital around the clock. All we could do was wait.

The next three days seemed to drag by. I don't remember doing much of anything. I just sat around the house most of the time. When I turned on the television, nothing ever appealed to me. And I didn't feel like going anywhere, because I didn't want to talk to anyone.

On Wednesday Jeremy asked if I wanted to play a game or something. I shrugged my shoulders when he suggested checkers. We played, but I couldn't concentrate and he beat me easily, even though I think he was trying to let me win. I didn't care whether I won or lost.

That afternoon the sky grew cloudy for the first time in over a week, and we had to turn the lights on in the living room. I was sitting in there when mother called the hospital. This time, Susan's condition was listed as "poor."

"She's not going to get better?" I said. Tears welled up in my eyes.

"I don't know," said Mother quietly. She reached out to comfort me, but I turned and went up to my room, even though it was stifling up there. I threw myself face down on my bed in the dim light and lay there a long time, crying and picking at the chenille bedspread. *Please God,* I prayed over and over, *don't let her die. Please God, not Susan! Not my best friend!*

Suddenly, a crack of thunder shook the house. I jumped up and ran over to the dormer window. Dark clouds were churning angrily in the sky. In the distance, jagged streaks of lightning flashed on and off, almost mechanically. When I looked down into the backyard, the leaves on the maple tree were flipped backward.

Huge raindrops started to slam against the upper window panes, thumping on the roof overhead. I knelt at the open window, crossed my arms on the sill, and laid my head on them. The wet breeze that filtered through the screen cooled my sweaty skin and dampened my hair. I stayed there for a long while with my eyes closed. I listened as the rain hammered on a tin roof next door, wishing I could make time stop and never go forward.

Chapter Twelve

Finally the rain softened, and I stood up and closed the window. I mopped up the window sill with a couple of tissues and tossed them in the wastebasket.

At about 5:30, my mother was shaping hamburger meat into patties, and I was listlessly setting dinner plates around the table when the phone rang. Mother couldn't answer with ground beef on her fingers, so I went in and picked up the receiver. It was Mrs. Cobb.

"Kathy?" she said. "Is your mother there?" Her voice sounded flat.

"Yes, but she can't come to the phone right now."

There was silence for a moment. Then she said, "Well . . . I just wondered whether you'd heard."

"Heard what?"

Silence again.

"Mrs. Cobb, heard what?" I said. I burst into tears. It was about Susan, I knew it. I wanted to hang up and run. Anywhere.

Fortunately, Mother came, drying her hands on her apron. She took the phone and sank down on the telephone bench. She listened a few moments, her expression unchanging and then she said quietly, "Yes, I'll tell her. Yes. All right. Thank you, Ethel."

Mother hung up the receiver. She didn't need to tell me. Susan was dead. Mrs. Cobb said it happened at four o'clock. It had been peaceful, and the Marshalls had been there with her.

The words bounced around the room, hitting me over and over again as they caromed back and forth. Susan, dead. Susan dead. Dead. I couldn't make sense of this thing that was tearing my world apart.

"No!" I cried. "No! It can't be!" I buried my face against my mother and felt her arms around me, hugging me tightly at first and then patting me like she used to when I was a little girl. I wanted her to rock me like she did then—when only goldfish died, and I'd never heard of anything called polio.

And on top of it was the unthinkable—that Susan would still be alive if I hadn't talked her into going swimming. This was all my fault.

Chapter 13

1952

After Susan's death, time fell into two parts for me: before she died, when almost every day was fun—and after she died, when guilt poisoned everything I did.

After the funeral I felt numb for days. The memory of Susan lying in that coffin haunted me, especially at night. Sometimes I woke up crying, but I never told anyone. My parents and my brother tiptoed around me the first couple of days, but later I noticed them watching me anxiously.

"Would you like to go shopping with me?" my mother would ask. Or Daddy would bring home something he knew I liked—a Hershey bar, maybe, or a record by Nat King Cole or Peggy Lee, my favorite singers. I knew they were trying to cheer me up, and I always thanked them, but it didn't really help.

A week after the funeral, I cleaned my room from top to bottom in spite of the heat. With a fan going, I took down the curtains and all the pictures and pennants I'd tacked on the walls. I washed the windows while the curtains flapped on the clothesline.

My mother was pleased to see all this, of course. "I'll iron the curtains," she said eagerly, as she lifted the ironing board from its corner alongside the refrigerator. So while Mother hummed and ironed downstairs, I silently scrubbed down the walls in my room.

The next day I cleaned out my closet, removing some outgrown stuff and arranging my shoes in a neat row on the floor. Back in the shadows, behind the shoes, lay Susan's rolled-up towel with her bathing suit inside. Just the sight of it made my stomach knot up. I knew I should get rid of them, but I didn't know how. I couldn't just put them in a wastebasket, because it was Jeremy's job to empty the trash, and he saw everything that went out of the house. I probably could have waited until no one was around and taken them to a public trash can, but somehow I wanted to keep them—at least at that point. Finally I stuffed them into my old navy blue gym bag. No one would ever look in there.

In the weeks that followed, I did everything my parents asked me to do just as soon as they asked, and I never once fought with Jeremy. Something deep inside wouldn't let me do otherwise.

"Well, Kathy," Daddy said one evening, when I carried a tray of iced tea into the living room. He set aside his newspaper. "You seem to have turned over a new leaf these days."

I smiled sweetly but didn't say anything. *If he only knew how hard I've been trying to seem good.*

Mother looked up from her needlework and smiled as she lifted a glass from the tray. "Your father's right," she said. "Your room is so neat and clean, and I really appreciate the way you've been helping me without even being asked. I guess that's called growing up." She winked at me, but then her smile faded. "I do wonder, though, why you still haven't talked to the Marshalls."

I shrugged. "It makes me sad to see them."

That didn't satisfy my mother. "The whole thing is sad, Kathy," she said, setting her glass down on the coffee table. "But think how the Marshalls must feel. Susan was their only child, you know."

I winced inwardly and said quietly, "I'll go soon." Then I changed the subject. "If it's okay with you, I think I'll get ready for bed."

Mother looked over at Daddy and raised her eyebrows. He glanced at his watch. "It's only 8:30," he said.

"I know, but I want to get back on schedule. School opens next week, you know."

"Sure, but we're the ones who usually have to tell you that," he said. They didn't know, though, how tired you can get pretending all the time. Pretending was the only way I could get through the days. Pretending that I was as mystified as everyone else as to how Susan—Susan alone of all the people I knew—could have caught polio. Pretending I was the good, obedient child everyone thought I was. Pretending I wasn't absolutely torn up inside by my guilt and loneliness. And knowing that I'd never, ever forgive myself for what I'd done.

❦ ❦ ❦

When school started in September, I wondered how I'd make it through the first few days. Everywhere I went, the kids kept talking about Susan—and especially about polio. "We're lucky school was out when she got sick," someone said. "We could've gotten it, too."

"You mean just by being around her?" said someone else.

"Sure. That's an epidemic for you."

They knew, of course, that I missed Susan, and they

told me they were sorry. But I never knew how lonely you can be even when you're surrounded by other kids.

Soon, though, everyone became busy with new things, like algebra and trying out for the talent show. "You going to audition?" asked Jeannie Grayson, falling into step next to me in the hallway. "I heard Kenny Goodwin's going to play his clarinet."

I looked straight ahead and kept walking. "Really?" I said, without any enthusiasm. "I hadn't thought about auditioning."

"You oughta. You and—Susan—used to sing really well together."

I felt my eyes filling up. "Thanks, Jeannie, but—well, I just I can't do that yet." I looked over at her. "Sing by myself, I mean."

"Sure, I know. But if you did, I bet they'd choose you!"

I couldn't imagine ever singing again. Not ever, when there was nothing to sing about. But I kept my smile on wherever I went. I guess that's why everyone thought I'd gotten over Susan. If they knew how awful I really felt inside, they might find out what the reason was.

When I wasn't at school, I was at home studying. My grades improved a little, mostly because I did all my homework, but sometimes in class when a teacher asked me a question, I would realize I hadn't heard it.

"What did you say?" I would ask. My cheeks would burn and turn red.

At first they'd just repeat the question, but as the weeks went by, I knew some of them were watching me. Finally, my English teacher stopped me one day on the way out of class.

"Kathy," she said, peering over her glasses, "you

don't seem to have your mind on your work this year."

I smiled weakly and shrugged, not knowing what to say.

"Is everything all right at home?" she asked quietly.

"Sure," I said. She didn't ask how I felt inside, and even if she had, I couldn't have told her anyway.

"Well, I hope you'll try harder to concentrate in class. Sometimes you seem to be a million miles away."

I smiled again and said I would try. And I did. But there was something cold and hard in the pit of my stomach that had become a part of me, reminding me all the time of July 18th—the day we went to the pool. The day NO ONE MUST EVER KNOW ABOUT.

🐞 🐞 🐞

One day near the end of September, Mother asked me to return a plate that Mrs. Morrison had left at the church. She lived just down the street. Jeremy wrinkled his nose. "Is she that funny old man's wife?"

"Funny?" asked Mother.

"Funny strange, I mean," said Jeremy. "He throws his garbage into his backyard."

"What?" I asked, amused.

"He does. Pete Jenkins lives behind him, and he says he's seen Mr. Morrison carry garbage out and dump it in the corner of his yard." Jeremy rolled his eyes. "He's strange."

I looked over at Mother. "Is he?"

Mother frowned. "I don't know much about Rodney Morrison. He seems nice enough at church. And his garden is the envy of the neighborhood."

She was right. The rosebushes around the Morrisons'

corner house were so thick you could hardly see their fence. We had only one little rosebush in our yard, and it hardly ever bloomed. My mother didn't like to garden, and my father was always too busy fixing up the house to do much more than that. They paid Jeremy to mow the lawn, which was mostly just crab grass anyway, according to Daddy.

When I went over to the Morrisons' and opened their gate, I stopped short. The yard inside was like a picture from a magazine. A lawn like a thick green rug encircled the house as far around as I could see. In the center, on the left, stood a white stone birdbath. The water inside sparkled in the sunlight. Birds were chirping in a willow tree in the corner, and some butterflies were chasing each other over a flower bed. Even though it was late in September, there were still lots of flowers blooming.

Two neatly trimmed bushes stood on either side of the front stoop, and two white stone planters on the steps were filled with white and purple flowers that spilled over the rims like a waterfall. Even the front walk had little white flowers growing along the edges.

Feeling almost like I was dreaming, I mounted the steps and pushed on the doorbell. As I waited for the door to open, I looked around, still enjoying the quiet beauty below. Then I rang the bell again. Still no answer.

Just as I turned to go back down the steps, an elderly man appeared from around the side yard. He was dressed in faded overalls and a flannel shirt. A wide-brimmed straw hat shaded his face.

"Hi, there!" he called, tilting his head up toward me. "Lookin' for the missus?"

I nodded. "Is she home?"

The man set down his bucket. "No," he said, smiling, "she's down at the hairdresser's. Should be back pretty soon, though. Can I help you?"

I smiled back at him and came down the steps.
"Well, my mother wanted me to return a plate Mrs.
Morrison left at church."

The man pulled off his hat. I recognized Mr.
Morrison then, right away. He just looked different when he
wasn't all dressed up. "Thanks so much, young lady," he
said, taking the plate from me. I liked the way his eyes
twinkled when he talked. "Mighty kind of you to bring it
over." He stood holding the plate and squinting in the late
afternoon sunlight. When he spoke again, his eyes met
mine, but his smile dropped just briefly. "You're the Jordan
girl, aren't you? I remember seeing you at the funeral."

For an awful second I wondered how much he
knew. "Yes," I said, as brightly as I could manage. "Name's
Kathy."

He nodded. "Well, Kathy. How would you like to
have some flowers for your trouble?"

"Oh, it was no trouble, Mr. Morrison," I said, shaking my head but hoping he'd give me some anyway.

Mr. Morrison started across the lawn. "No point in
growing flowers if you don't share 'em," he said.

I followed him past the birdbath and over to one of
the flower beds. "This sure is a beautiful yard," I said.

He didn't answer. He was busy clipping off some big
yellow and orange flowers—the kind ladies sometimes
wear to football games. He handed them to me. "If you like
my yard, you'll like my mums."

"Is that what these are called?" I said, as I cradled
them. I had never held such huge flowers.

Mr. Morrison smiled again. "They're really called
chrysanthemums, but I like nicknames, don't you?"

"Sure," I said, grinning.

Then he picked some red-orange flowers on tall, thin stalks—scarlet sage, he said they were—and some other yellow ones that were smaller than the mums.

"Those are asters," he said, handing them to me, "and here are a few roses. Not too many left this time of year."

Roses! My favorite flower. I bent my head down, enjoying the fragrance. Then I looked up at him gratefully. "I love flowers—especially roses," I said.

When he heard that, he asked if I'd ever grown any flowers.

"Me? I wouldn't know how."

"Well, I'll teach you. Come back tomorrow, and I'll give you a lesson."

I shifted the bouquet a bit and said, "Sure, if it's okay with my mother." It sounded like fun. And for the first time in two months, I had almost forgotten the awful pain inside me.

Chapter 14

1952

Mr. Morrison gave me my first gardening lesson the very next day. He told me again the names of the flowers he'd picked the afternoon before. It was a good thing he did, because when I brought them home I couldn't remember what the red ones were called, and my mother didn't know either. Mr. Morrison named all the other flowers in the garden, and he showed me which ones had bloomed all summer and which flowers bloomed only in the fall. "If you plan carefully," he said, "you can have flowers in Maryland from early spring until Jack Frost comes around late in October."

I guess my mother was glad I was finally interested in something other than school work, for she quickly agreed that I could go there whenever it was all right with Mr. Morrison. She probably thought, too, that it was time *someone* in the family learned something about gardening. But what I liked best was that the only things he and I—or Mrs. Morrison, whenever she was around—ever talked about were flowers and gardening. No questions to answer. No need to pretend.

When I arrived one afternoon in early October, the

sun was filtering down through the yellow leaves of the trees, and overhead the sky was a brilliant blue. Mr. Morrison waved to me from across the lawn. He pointed to a lumpy burlap bag in the wheelbarrow he'd been pushing. "You're just in time, Kathy," he said. "Guess what I've got."

I peered into the open bag. "Onions?" I asked.

He chuckled. "Look like onions, don't they? They're tulip bulbs."

"Tulip bulbs!"

"Yep, and we're going to plant 'em all around that little tree over there."

I soon learned, though, that there was a lot more to planting tulips than just digging holes and sticking the bulbs down into the ground. Mr. Morrison explained that we had to prepare the soil.

"What do you mean, 'prepare' it?" I asked.

He took off his cap and scratched his head. "Well, plants are kind of like people," he said. "They need sunshine, food and water, and a good place to grow." Then he told me that a good way to give tulip bulbs food was by adding bone meal to the soil.

"What's that?" I asked.

"Ground-up bones is all," he said, with a twinkle in his eye.

I shuddered. "And that makes tulips grow better?"

"Best thing for 'em!"

I glanced around at the garden. "Did you use bone meal to grow all these flowers?" I asked.

Mr. Morrison picked up a trowel and started digging. "I used compost for the others," he said.

"What's that?"

"Oh, just some stuff I mix up out back." He and I got busy then, digging the holes and pouring the bone meal deep into each one. Before we put the tulip bulbs in, though, he showed me which end of the bulb was which. "Make sure you put 'em in with the top up," he said, chuckling, "or they'll come up in China instead of Maryland!"

When we were finished, he let me push the wheelbarrow around to the back of the house, where the tool shed was. While he was putting the wheelbarrow away, I noticed a big pile of dirt next to the shed. It was fenced in with chicken wire almost as high as I was. When I got up closer, though, I saw that the pile was more than dirt. There were dark gray leaves in there and . . . "Yikes!" I shrieked, jumping back. A little snake had slithered out from the bottom.

Mr. Morrison poked his head out of the shed.

The snake darted over to the shed. "A snake!" I said, pointing. "It's over there."

He looked, and then he smiled. "Just one of God's little creatures," he chuckled. "Won't hurt you."

I winced.

Mr. Morrison stood back, with his thumbs tucked into his overall pockets. "All kinds of little critters get into compost," he said.

"This is compost?" I wasn't so sure I'd want to use it.

"Yep! Made it myself. Learned how when I was stationed in England during the First World War. To the English, you know, beautiful gardens and compost piles go hand in hand."

"How do you make it?"

"Well, you start with garbage."

"Garbage?" I stiffened, remembering what Jeremy had said about Mr. Morrison a few weeks earlier.

"Yep! Raw food scraps that most people just throw away—like potato or carrot peelings. Coffee grounds are good too. Just about anything . . .but no meat scraps. "

I leaned cautiously toward the bin. I didn't want to meet any more of his "critters." "I don't see any garbage," I said.

"Oh, it's there, all right, but it's all covered up." Mr. Morrison bent down and pointed near the bottom of the compost pile. "First there are leaves and grass clippings, then the garbage and a little manure . . ."

I wrinkled my nose. "Manure?"

"Wonderful for growing things."

I well remembered the smell of manure from visiting my uncle's farm in Illinois. I was puzzled, though. "How come this doesn't smell bad?" I asked.

Mr. Morrison smiled and said, "If a compost pile gets plenty of air—like this one does—you won't smell the manure or the garbage."

He explained that next came fertilizer and then a couple of inches of dirt. "I keep repeating the layers until the bin's filled. When I'm finished, I press down on the top with a shovel so the rain will soak in. You have to keep it moist, you see." He stood admiring it, with his arms crossed.

"And so that's how you make compost?" I asked.

"That's only how you start it. God takes care of the rest . . . all in His time."

"God?"

"Sure enough. It'll decompose over the next few months. And by planting time in the spring, it'll be ready to work its wonders!"

I stood chewing my knuckle while Mr. Morrison locked up the shed. When he came back, I said, "That's funny."

"Yeah?"

"Most of the stuff you use for compost is ugly and no good

for anything. I mean, you'd just throw it away otherwise."

Mr. Morrison nodded.

"And yet," I continued, "it can make something beautiful like flowers!"

"Yep! That's why some people call it 'black gold.'"

It wasn't long before I began to wish we could plant a garden in our yard. My dad said it was fine with him, as long as I knew what to do and how to do it. He helped me pick out some bulbs at a nursery, and he even dug up a place in the front yard so we could get started. Mr. Morrison brought over a bag of bone meal, and the three of us planted daffodils, tulips, and even a rose bush. And before he left that day, Mr. Morrison said that when spring came, he'd give us some compost for the plants that grow from seeds. I was going to have a garden!

❦ ❦ ❦

At school, things went on pretty much as they had been before I met the Morrisons. I studied hard and kept my smile on, but usually I kept pretty much to myself. And everywhere I went, I missed Susan. I missed her during homeroom, remembering how we used to joke around before our first class. I missed her at lunch time, when we always sat together. And I think I missed her most after school, when we used to walk home together. Now I usually walked home alone, crying sometimes as I remembered Susan and me waiting for each other after school. We'd go over all the things that happened that day. And then we'd often call each other up as soon as we got home because we'd forgotten to tell each other something—something funny, most of the time. I wondered if I'd ever be able to laugh again.

By late October I still hadn't talked to either of Susan's parents. I felt bad about that, but at the same time, I was glad I hadn't had to face them. One Sunday, though, just as I was leaving the ladies' room at church, Mrs. Marshall came in the door.

Chapter 15

1952

Both Mrs. Marshall and I stopped, surprised. She looked thinner than she used to, and there were tired lines around her eyes. Her smile, though, was still just as warm as always.

"Why, Kathy," she said, "it's good to see you."

I smiled back and cleared my throat. "Same here," I said, frantically wondering what to say next.

"How are you doing, dear?"

"Pretty good, thanks. How about you?"

"Fine, just fine." She looked away. "It's been hard, of course."

"Oh, I know," I said quickly, wanting to hug her and yet run out the door at the same time. I stood there awkwardly for a moment, and then I said, "Well, I guess I'd better get to my class." As I turned to leave, I added, "It was good to see you again."

"Of course." Mrs. Marshall nodded soberly, watching as I opened the door. As I did, I looked back and said softly, "I really miss Susan."

Mrs. Marshall's eyes filled up. "I know you do, dear."

Then I left. I left without saying any more than that. I didn't tell her I thought of Susan every hour of every day, and that for the rest of my life I would hate myself for causing her daughter's death.

I had a hard time concentrating in Sunday School class. I kept thinking about Mrs. Marshall, wondering if I would ever be able to talk to her—really talk, as we used to.

Mrs. Gibson, our teacher, had us take turns reading Psalm 139. Usually, whenever we read something out of the Bible, I thought about people who lived thousands of years ago. But that day the verses leaped up from the page and terrified me.

Sandy Collins, who sat next to me, was asked to read first. "O Lord," she began, "thou hast searched me and known me! Thou knowest when I sit down and when I rise up; thou discernest my thoughts from afar."

I felt my face turning red.

She read on: "Whither shall I go from thy Spirit? Or whither shall I flee from thy presence?"

My eyes started to fill with tears. I knew I'd never be able to hold back for long, so I got up and left, closing the door behind me. I grabbed my coat from the rack in the empty hallway, but just as I turned to leave, the classroom door flew open and Mrs. Gibson came out. "Kathy," she said, "what's wrong?"

"Nothing. I just need to go somewhere. See you next week."

I ran down the hall, out of the building, and across the street. I was still fighting back my tears, and I wanted desperately to go home. But if my parents hadn't left for church yet, there'd be questions—lots of them.

I slipped down a side street and kept walking.
Where could I go? I wished I was invisible. If any people
from church saw me, they'd wonder why I wasn't in
Sunday School, and if they saw me crying . . . Fortunately,
no one was around.

After a while I turned a corner and saw the
Morrisons' house down at the end of the block. When I got
closer, I could see that their car wasn't in the driveway. I
stopped at the front gate, wishing I could go in. Would I be
trespassing if I did—while they were at church? I waited a
moment, and then I slipped inside.

The same feeling of peacefulness that I always felt in
their yard swept over me when I saw the thick lawn and the
nodding flowers that Mr. Morrison tended so carefully. I
hurried over to the willow tree and sank down, leaning
wearily against the trunk. Now the tears I had fought so
long could roll down my cheeks, and no one would know
or care. . . .

I don't know how long I had sat there crying when I
heard a screen door slam. I looked up. Mr. Morrison was
coming across the yard, lugging a large plastic bucket. He
didn't see me at first, and I wondered if I could sneak out. I
froze for a few seconds. No use. Almost as soon as he
looked up, he saw me. He seemed surprised, but he smiled.

"Well, look who's here!" he said, dumping the con-
tents of the bucket onto his compost pile.

"Hi, Mr. Morrison," I said weakly, wishing I could
drop through a trap door or something. "I thought you
were at church."

He smiled. "I had a headache when I woke up, so
the missus went by herself." He walked back over toward
me. "How about you? No Sunday School today?"

I dropped my eyes. "There was, but I didn't stay." A

tear rolled down to the end of my nose, and I swished it away with the back of my hand. I looked up at him. "Hope you don't mind that I came in here," I said, sniffing. "I just needed a quiet place."

"Fine with me," said Mr. Morrison, handing me a clean white handkerchief. He flipped his empty bucket over and eased himself down onto it. "Troubles?" he asked.

I nodded and sniffed again.

He nodded back and just sat quietly, looking out across the lawn. Somewhere above us a cardinal was singing. Mr. Morrison had taught me how to pick out the cardinal's song from other birds'.

I sat folding and refolding his handkerchief. Finally I said, "How can it be so beautiful outside when I feel so terrible inside?"

Mr. Morrison looked at me. "That bad, huh?"

"Worse than you can imagine."

He smiled slightly. "Well, I don't know. I've known some pretty terrible things in my day too."

"But this is something I did. Something that was my fault." Tears started rolling down my cheeks again.

He nodded slowly. "Most of us do some pretty bad things once in a while, you know."

"Not like this. This is the worst."

Mr. Morrison sat quietly for a while, and then he stood up and rubbed at the back of his neck slowly. "Kathy, you might not believe this, but somebody would be alive today if it weren't for me."

Something like an electric current surged through me. I couldn't believe what I'd just heard. I couldn't say anything—I just sat there, frozen, wide-eyed.

He looked far off. For a moment I thought he might not say any more. Then he said, "It was back during World

War I—in France. My buddy Tom and I had been in a trench for about thirty hours straight, wondering when we'd ever be able to move on. I was sick of war, sick of the killing. We were both exhausted, and deep down inside I was scared to death. It had been my job to run over to the next platoon with messages whenever someone brought one to us—we didn't have radios then, you know." He paused, and it was almost as if he were talking to himself. "Well, finally word came that the Germans were advancing, and we were to be on the alert. I was supposed to warn the others.

"I don't know what happened to me then, but I sort of snapped, I guess—started crying, in fact. 'I can't do it again!' I said. 'I can't go over there. I'll get killed this time, I know I will!'

"And then Tom—my best buddy—said, 'Never mind, Rodney, I'll go.' And before I could stop him, he crawled out and tried to make it over to the others.

"'Tom!' I yelled. 'Wait!'" Mr. Morrison paused. "He never made it," he said quietly, blinking back his tears. "I just thank the good Lord he never knew what hit him." He sat shaking his head.

I swallowed hard, wanting to say something, but I couldn't.

"After that, I lost all interest in everything and everyone. They called it 'shell shock,' but it was really a broken heart." He stopped, and again I didn't know what to say. It didn't matter, because he wasn't finished. "Eventually," he said, "we were shipped home, and for the next year all I could think about was Tom: him dead and me alive. It about tore me apart. . . ."

He stopped and looked at me, and his eyes were so sad I almost started crying again. "You see," he said, "I do know what it's like to feel terrible inside yourself."

"But then, what happened?" I said quickly. "I mean, you seem to be okay now."

"Well, in time I knew in my head it wasn't my fault that Tom got killed, but I just couldn't forgive myself."

Tears were running down my cheeks again, and I just sat there feeling limp.

Mr. Morrison continued. "What finally helped, though, was the garden," he said.

"The garden?"

He nodded. "Planting one and then working in it. My minister suggested it. Said it might help get my mind off my troubles. What I found, though, was a way to forgive myself."

"What do you mean?" I leaned forward.

"Well, as bad as the old memories were, I soon found that helping young plants to grow brought me a sense of peace I hadn't found anywhere else. And I was finally doing something besides just kicking myself." Mr. Morrison stood up then and leaned a hand against the willow tree as he looked out at his garden. "When I think about it," he continued, "what God did with my life was a lot like composting."

I raised my eyebrows. "Composting?"

There were tears in his eyes again, but this time he was smiling. "Yep," he said, "He took all that guilt and made it into something useful, just like composting does for soil."

I needed to get on my way shortly after that, but before I left I said to him, "I'm awfully glad you came back from the war."

He grinned. "That's what my wife says, too."

As I walked back home, I thought about all that Mr.

Chapter Fifteen

Morrison and I had talked about, and especially what he'd said about composting. If something as beautiful as his garden could come from that awful time in his life, I decided then maybe something good can come out of mine. And if God could help Mr. Morrison forgive himself, maybe He could help me, too.

I smiled and started humming. And for the first time since Susan died, the tightness in my stomach started to go away.

Chapter 16

1952

I was glad no one was home when I got back to the house. I let myself in with my key and closed the front door firmly. I could smell the roast Mother had put into the oven before she left for church—part of her Sunday morning ritual. The Sunday paper was spread around the floor by my dad's chair in the deserted living room. In the kitchen, Mother had cleared the breakfast table, and the dishes, washed and rinsed, were drying in the dish rack.

I drew a glass of water and stood looking out the kitchen window after I drank it. A large cloud had cast a shadow over everything in the backyard, even though off in the distance the sun was sparkling on some windows behind our house. As I watched, though, the cloud slid sideways, and suddenly our yard was bathed in sunlight. *That's like me!* I thought. *Everything in my life was cloudy until Mr. Morrison told me his story. Now I feel like the sun is finally coming out.*

I always change my clothes right after church, and I

did that day too. I put on my favorite outfit—blue jeans rolled up to the knees, one of my dad's old white shirts, and my saddle shoes. I smiled as I dressed, remembering how long it had taken my mother to get used to seeing me in these clothes, especially if I planned to go anywhere.

"Aren't you at least going to tuck in your shirttail?" she had asked the first time.

I'd rolled my eyes. "No one tucks in their shirttails, Mother."

"Well, you look like a ragamuffin!" she'd said, with her hands on her hips.

"No, I don't. Everyone looks like this."

"That's what I mean. You *all* look like ragamuffins!"

I was certain that my mother was hopelessly behind the times.

As I hung up my dress, I started rehearsing in my mind what I'd tell my parents when they came home and wanted to know where I'd been. I'd tell them . . . My eyes fell on the gym bag that still lay in a back corner of my closet. It had been in there almost three months by then. I bent down and touched it gingerly, as if it might explode or something. Carefully, I picked it up and carried it out of the closet.

I laid the bag on my bed and sat down beside it. Slowly, gently, I pulled out the towel and unrolled it—and there was the turquoise bathing suit that Susan had worn the last day we were together. My eyes filled up at the sight of it. I could still see Susan poised at edge of the pool, then splashing down next to me in the water, and, finally, giggling as we tried frantically to dry our suits with my hair dryer before my mother came home.

As I sat looking at it, I thought of the psalm Sandy Collins had been reading when I ran out of Sunday School that morning: "O Lord, thou has searched me and known me . . . thou discernest my thoughts from afar."

I shook my head, wondering for the thousandth time what God must think if He knows "my thoughts from afar." *But at least,* I thought, *He also knows how sorry I am.*

I picked up Susan's bathing suit and hugged it. *Oh Susan,* I thought, *do you know, too? Do you know that I never wanted this to happen? I miss you so much!* Tears were streaming down my cheeks.

Suddenly, I couldn't stand it any longer—not one more day of pretending. No matter what else happened, I knew I had to tell. I looked up at the bulletin board over my bed. It was covered with snapshots of my family and my friends, full of smiling faces and arms around each other. What would they think when they found out? Would anybody still like me? Or worse—would anybody still *love* me?

Just then I heard the front door open and, a few moments later, my mother's voice: "Kathy?"

I bit my lip. "I'm up here," I called.

Then I heard my dad at the foot of the steps. "You all right, honey?"

"I guess so," I said. I grabbed the suit and towel, took a deep breath, and headed for the stairs.

My parents were standing at the foot of the steps, and they saw right away that I'd been crying.

"What in the world happened to you?" mother said. "You were supposed to be helping out in the church nursery, and we heard after church that you left in the middle of Sunday School!"

The nursery! I had forgotten all about it! "Oh, I'm sorry," I said, clapping my hands to my face. My eyes filled up again.

Daddy slipped his arm around me and led me over

to the couch. I laid my head against his chest and cried, hard this time. Mother settled in a chair next to us and leaned close. "Whatever it is, you can tell us, honey," she said gently. Then she noticed the bathing suit. "What's that?" she asked, looking at it curiously.

The question had finally come, as I knew it would sooner or later. I worked to get the words out: "It's—it's Susan's bathing suit."

"Susan's?" My mother pulled back just a little. "What's it doing at our house?"

"She left it here."

"When?"

I lowered my eyes and said slowly, "The last time she was over. It's been in my closet ever since."

"Your closet?"

I sighed and decided to start at the beginning. I looked from one of my parents to the other, took a deep breath and began. "Remember how hot it was last summer?" I said.

Daddy leaned back. "Hottest on record," he said.

"Well, one Friday in July, I was so bored. There was absolutely nothing to do. Jeremy had gone to Washington, and Mother, you were at the rummage sale. . . ."

My mother shifted a little in her chair and glanced at Daddy. Then she said, "But I let you have Susan over for lunch that day, remember?"

I nodded. I knew I was going to have to choose the next words carefully. "Well," I said, "remember how you both had said we couldn't go to the pool anymore?"

They nodded, looking at me gravely.

I sat up a little straighter. "I really thought that was unfair," I said, glancing at each of them. "I mean, I thought we ought to have just one more chance to swim."

Chapter Sixteen

Daddy narrowed his eyes just a little. "So you went anyway," he said quietly.

I bit my lip. "Both of us did," I said, looking squarely at him, "but I was the one who talked Susan into going." I could feel a lump forming in my throat.

Neither of them said anything. They just sat there listening.

"It wasn't much fun that day," I continued. "Hardly anyone was at the pool, so we left early." I told how we'd tried to dry our suits with my new hair dryer, but we finally gave up and left them hanging in my closet.

"And Susan never took hers home," said Mother, shifting again in her chair.

"It was still damp," I explained. "I was going to take it back when I stayed overnight the next week, but I never . . ." Remembering how sick Susan had become just a few days later, my eyes filled up. "Oh, Mother—Daddy! I'm so sorry! I didn't mean for her to catch polio!"

My dad put his arms around me again and held me while I sobbed against his chest. After a few moments, I heard him say softly to Mother, "All this time she's been blaming herself for Susan's death!"

I pulled back and wiped my tears with the back of my hand. "But she'd still be alive if it weren't for . . ."

"Don't say that, Kathy!" said Mother. "No one knows what causes polio."

I looked at her. "But everyone says you can get it in swimming pools!"

Daddy shook his head. "That's mostly guesswork, Kathy. Someday scientists may find out what causes it, but nobody knows at this point."

I nodded.

Mother took my hands in hers. She looked hard into

my eyes and spoke slowly. "Sometimes," she said, "people have come down with polio after swimming, but that doesn't mean that Susan necessarily caught it at the pool." She hesitated a moment, and then she raised her voice. "You mustn't blame yourself, Kathy!"

I watched her pleading eyes, and for a fraction of a second I hoped she was right. When I was little, I thought my mother knew everything. Maybe she did now, too. Maybe Susan really had caught polio somewhere else—on another day. But then the old thoughts returned. I pulled my hands away. "But we'll never know!" I insisted.

Daddy said, "You're right, Kathy. We'll never know, so blaming yourself really isn't fair, is it?" He patted my arm and said, a little louder, "And it won't bring Susan back."

I sniffed and nodded.

Mother jumped up. "The roast!" she said, hurrying into the kitchen. I noticed then that the smell of meat roasting had changed to meat scorching.

A few moments later she called from the kitchen, asking if we could continue our talk at dinner. I quickly agreed and got up to set the table, glad to be thinking about other things for a while. I was relieved, too, when Jeremy called for permission to stay at a friend's for dinner. *It will still be just the three of us*, I thought gratefully.

After my father said grace and we had passed the food, there was silence around the table. I sat carefully cutting my meat, wondering what to say next, when Daddy cleared his throat. "I guess I don't have to tell you, Kathy, that you were wrong to disobey us and go swimming that day."

I kept my eyes on my plate. "I know."

He reached for the salt and continued, "But you have to

remember that Susan disobeyed her parents that day too." He looked over at me and said, "You didn't force Susan to do anything, did you." He said it as a fact, not as a question.

"No," I said softly.

And Mother said, "Susan made a choice, just like you did."

Daddy set the salt shaker down and looked at me. I'll never forget how gently he spoke. "Sometimes," he said, "kids do things together that they'd never think of doing by themselves."

There was another long silence after that. This time, though, I was thinking about my parents and how I never knew when I had loved them so much. Or felt their love so much, either. *In spite of everything,* I thought, *I must be one of the luckiest kids around.*

But there was one more thing: I still had to face the Marshalls.

Chapter 17

1952

After dinner I helped Mother with the dishes, and then I stayed up in my room for a while, rehearsing in my mind what I might say to Susan's parents. I tried different ways to start out: "Mrs. Marshall," (or Mr. Marshall—whoever opened the door) "can I come in? I need to talk to you about something important." Jake would probably be there wagging his tail when the door opened—that is, if he still remembered me.

They'd ask me in and probably ask me to sit down right there in the living room. Then I'd choose a chair—maybe the one with the crocheted doilies on the arms and another doily on the back for your head. Mrs. Marshall might offer me a glass of soda or something.

And what would I say next? I wondered. Something like, "I've been meaning to come and see you . . . I guess you've wondered why I took so long, but, you see, I've been really busy with school and all. . . ."

The Marshalls' house was always quiet compared to

ours. My father was always fixing something, and if he wasn't hammering, he'd keep the radio going nearby.

I wondered if Mr. Marshall would be sitting in that chair, doing his crossword puzzle. He always used to work on the one in the Sunday paper while Mrs. Marshall and Susan got dinner ready, and later he'd finish it in time to watch "Lassie" with Susan at seven o'clock. I used to like to watch that show with them sometimes, even though their screen was smaller than ours. Just remembering those evenings made my eyes fill up. . . .

I carefully prepared in my mind's eye the conversation we would have. Somehow I'd manage to tell them everything. And when I was finished, the secret would be out. No more games with anyone and, hopefully, no more need to avoid the Marshalls. But would we ever really be friends again?

I moved to my little dormer window. From up there, now that most of the leaves had blown off the trees, I could easily see the Marshalls' green roof in the distance. Were they there in the house this afternoon? And what do they talk about now that Susan's gone? Do they ever talk about me? Or worse—would they even want to talk to me after today? I looked at my watch. Better go and get it over with.

In a few minutes I was downstairs, pulling my jacket from the living room closet. Daddy was holding his newspaper open, and Mother had some crocheting in her hands, but I knew they were watching me as I crossed the room. "I'm going out for awhile," I said. I paused at the front door to take a deep breath.

"Out?" said Mother.

I turned and looked at them. "Over to the Marshalls'," I said, cracking my knuckles. "I've got to do it sometime."

Chapter Seventeen

They both smiled warmly. "Good for you, Kath," said Daddy.

"Want either of us to go with you?" my mother asked.

I shook my head. "No thanks," I said, and I closed the door behind me. *I can do it myself,* I thought. *I can. I have to.*

The few blocks down to the Marshalls' that day was the longest walk I ever took. And yet, I would have liked it to go on forever—anything rather than arrive at their doorstep.

I went out of my way a little in order to pass the Morrisons' house on my way to the Marshalls'. I paused slightly when I got there. The sight of Mr. Morrison's gold and purple chrysanthemums just inside the fence made me want like anything to dart inside and escape what lay ahead. I turned away, though, and continued walking down the street.

It was Mrs. Marshall who answered the door. She looked just as she had that same morning at church—tired, but pleased to see me. She stepped aside to let me in. Jake nuzzled up against me, wagging his tail furiously. I bent down and stroked him several times and then straightened up. My mind searched frantically for my carefully chosen words, but they were gone. "Mrs. Marshall," I blurted out, "I have to talk to you. . . ." I could feel tears starting, and her arms were instantly around me. We hugged each other for a long while.

When I finally stood back, Mr. Marshall was there next to us. He hugged me, too, awkwardly, and when we let go, there were tears in his eyes, too.

We all sat down, and I told them why I had come. I told them everything—the words came tumbling out. I hardly dared look at them, knowing what they must be thinking.

Mr. Marshall sat quietly next to me on the couch as I talked, so I couldn't see his face. Mrs. Marshall, across from me, sat twisting her handkerchief or dabbing at her eyes. She glanced at her husband several times as she listened. But, to my surprise, she never looked angry—just sad.

When I finished, we all sat there for a few minutes. I could hear the clock ticking across the room. Finally, Mrs. Marshall spoke up. "And all this time, Kathy, you've been afraid to tell us."

I nodded and sniffed.

She shifted in her chair and leaned forward. "I guess it's time I said something here."

I bit my lip and lowered my head, dreading what that might be.

She cleared her throat. "Susan had already told me all this," she said.

"What?" said Mr. Marshall softly. I could feel my breath stop in my throat.

She continued. "It was the day after she went into the hospital. I got there before you did that time, Paul, remember?"

He nodded.

Mrs. Marshall paused and rubbed her forehead, then she continued. "Well, Susan seemed restless and said she needed to talk to me. It's a good thing she did, because by the next day they had to put her in the iron lung . . ." Her eyes filled up. I couldn't even imagine Susan lying attached to a machine that breathed for her.

"She asked if I thought people caught polio from being in swimming pools. She'd asked me that before, and I said again that nobody really knows. That's when she told me about . . ." Mrs. Marshall choked on the words, "about her last day with you."

I sat staring down at my hands. "I've wished a thousand times," I said, shaking my head, "that I could live that day over again." I looked up at her and pleaded, "Do you think you can ever forgive me?"

Mrs. Marshall smiled faintly. "Kathy," she said, "Susan once told me she'd never had such a good friend as you were. We know you would never have done anything to deliberately hurt our daughter."

Mr. Marshall nodded in agreement. "We don't want to lose Susan and you, too, Kathy!"

I started crying then and went over and hugged each of them hard. The closeness I felt with them that day was something I'd never known before and have never needed since. Suddenly, I knew it was over at last—all the pain and the guilt I'd been feeling for what had seemed forever.

Finally, I dropped my arms and said, "I guess I'd better get going."

"I'm so glad you came," said Mr. Marshall, wiping his eyes.

"Please come again soon," said his wife, giving me another quick hug.

"I will," I said eagerly, "and thanks for letting me talk." And before I stepped outside they praised me for my courage in coming to them. My courage!

On the walk back to my house, I felt as if I had springs on my feet. If I'd been a little kid, I'd have skipped the whole way home.

I went by the Morrisons' once more, though. I stopped by the gate again and stood looking at the yard. The flowers, fading but still beautiful in the autumn twilight, reminded me once more of what Mr. Morrison had done with his life. And I thought, too, about Charles Wesley and all the hymns he'd written after he'd felt forgiven. And I knew then that I could go ahead and make something of my life. I might not be able to write a thousand hymns or grow such perfect flowers, but I decided then and there that if I did raise special flowers, they'd be roses. And if those roses could show how much I'd been forgiven by God, the Marshalls, and—incredibly—even myself, then I would probably plant a whole field of them!

History in Real Life:
Poliomyelitis—Polio

Poliomyelitis is a disease with a long name and a very long history of killing or crippling children and adults, especially in the summertime. As far back as the 1770s, polio, as it is called for short, may have been well known in Britain. Sir Walter Scott, a famous writer of that time, told of a fever that had left him lame when he was only 18 months old.

Medical books first described polio in 1879, but well into the twentieth century its cause and cure remained a mystery. A newspaper in 1916 claimed it was spread by "dogs, cats, and doctors' beards." The truth was, though, that no one knew what caused the disease, nor how to cure it.

By the mid-1930s, there had been several terrifying outbreaks of polio in the United States. Newspapers carried headlines about the number of cases reported, in what neighborhoods the patients lived, how many children had died, and how many others would never be able to walk again.

The two most serious kinds of polio, "bulbar" and "bulbar-spinal," caused damage to the nerves that control breathing and swallowing. During the 1940s and early '50s, newsreels and television newscasts showed row upon row of iron lungs—mechanical breathing tanks into which many persons with polio were placed, with their faces reflected in the mirrors attached above them.

Although polio was highly contagious, almost everyone who caught it recovered. Many were helped by a treatment devised by an Australian nurse named Sister Kenny. Her method of using hot, moist cloths to help muscles to work again was never fully accepted by many doctors. On the other hand, no one else was able to do much more than that for those who had been crippled by the disease.

Rumors and hysteria made polio appear much more deadly than it was. Parents kept their children away from crowds in the summertime. Hardly anyone attended Saturday matinees at movie theaters, and dust blew across empty ball fields. The places feared most, though, were swimming pools. Everyone knew that swimming in water used by others had often made people come down with polio, especially by the end of the summer. Swimming holes and community pools were either officially closed or abandoned by late July or early August.

All through the first half of the twentieth century, a few medical researchers were quietly and persistently working to discover how to cure polio or, better still, how to prevent it. Research, though, required a great deal of money, and there had been little to spare in the United States during the early years of the Depression.

Then in 1938, President Franklin D. Roosevelt, who had caught polio as a young man and had spent many years in a wheelchair, decided to do something to fight the disease. He established the National Foundation for Infantile Paralysis (yet another name for poliomyelitis) to encourage research. The work was supported by the March of Dimes, a campaign that raised much money, mostly from dimes collected in movie theaters. Everyone hoped that at last a cure would be found.

Another interruption followed, however, when the United States became involved in World War II in 1941. Many researchers were drafted into the armed services, causing their work to be postponed as the country concentrated its money and effort on winning the war.

Finally in 1947, polio research was begun again. Seven years later, in 1954, Dr. Jonas Salk developed the first tests of a polio vaccine. This led to the successful immunization of thousands of children. Just two years earlier, in 1952 (when *Gold in the Garden* takes place), the United States had suffered the worst polio epidemic in history, with 21,269 cases nationwide. By 1965, however, because most children were being given the vaccine, the number dropped to sixty-one.

Today we know that polio is an acute viral infection. Where it does still occur, it is spread by direct contact, especially where hygiene is poor. No medicine has ever been found to cure it, but because polio can now be prevented, it is hoped that this tragic disease will someday disappear from the face of the earth.

Read More about It

To find out more about poliomyelitis, check your local library for these titles:

Fiction

Johnston, Julie. *Hero of Lesser Causes*. Boston: Little, Brown, 1993.
In 1946, twelve-year-old Keely's older brother, Patrick, is paralyzed by polio. She starts a campaign to lift his spirits and bring some happiness to his life.

Nonfiction

Cohen, Daniel. *Vaccination and You*. New York: J. Messner, 1969.
Discusses the causes of diseases such as small pox, diphtheria, polio, and measles, and how vaccinations work.

Crofford, Emily. *Healing Warrior: A Story about Sister Elizabeth Kenny*. Minneapolis: Carolrhoda Books, 1989.
A biography of the Australian nurse who developed a successful method of treating and rehabilitating polio patients.

Curson, Marjorie. *Jonas Salk*. Englewood Cliffs, N.J.: Silver Burdett, 1990.
A biography of the scientist who developed a vaccine that conquered polio.

Duden, Jane. *1950s*. New York: Crestwood House, 1990.
> History, trivia, and fun through photographs and articles of life in the United States between 1950 and 1959.

Hargrove, Jim. *The Story of Jonas Salk and the Discovery of the Polio Vaccine*. Chicago: Children's Press, 1990.
> Recounts the successful search of Jonas Salk for the vaccine that conquered polio.

Harris, Nathaniel. *The Forties and Fifties: An Illustrated History in Colour, 1945-1959*. London: Macdonald and Co., 1975.
> Illustrated history of the fifteen years immediately after World War II. This book covers such topics as sports, fashions, movies, cars, and scientific developments (including the polio vaccine).

Krull, Kathleen. *Wilma Unlimited: How Wilma Rudolph became the World's Fastest Woman*. San Diego: Harcourt Brace, 1996.
> A biography of the African-American woman who overcame crippling polio as a child to become the first woman to win three gold medals in track in a single Olympics.

Lindop, Edmund. *An Album of the Fifties*. New York: Watts, 1978.
> Presents the issues and lifestyles of the 1950s in the United States.

About the Author

Dorothy Lilja Harrison has loved hearing and reading stories ever since she was a little girl. Later, when she grew up and had two boys and two girls of her own, she shared her love of books with her children, as well as with the kindergartners she taught. Now, she has taken that love to the next level—she has authored the Chronicles of Courage series.

During Mrs. Harrison's childhood, and when her first two children were very young, thousands became disabled or died during polio epidemics, just as in this story about Kathy Gordon and Susan Marshall. She wrote *Gold in the Garden* to help today's children appreciate the polio vaccine, which now prevents their catching this terrible disease. She also wrote the book to assure children that no matter what they've done, God still loves them and will forgive them if they are truly sorry.

Today Mrs. Harrison lives in Ellicott City, Maryland, with her husband, a retired United Methodist pastor. Their grown children have become a musician, an artist, an editor, and a nurse. Their two grandchildren live nearby.

A Better Tomorrow?

A snake in the kitchen?!

It seems the perfect revenge, but Janet's not sure she should go through with it.

Before the Depression, the Larsons had their own house and yard and were able to play with their friends whenever they wanted. Now Janet and her family are living with a cranky older woman named Mrs. Cooper who doesn't seem to like kids. She has very strict rules about having friends over, which hasn't made it easy for Janet to make new friends. She's tired of Mrs. Cooper and her rules, and she just wants to get even. But what does God want her to do?

Janet knows the Depression won't last forever, that God will bring a better tomorrow and she will have friends again. She just doesn't expect Mrs. Cooper to be one of them.

Be sure to read all three books in the
Chronicles of Courage series:
A Better Tomorrow?
Operation Morningstar
Gold in the Garden

Chariot VICTOR
◆ P U B L I S H I N G ◆
A DIVISION OF COOK COMMUNICATIONS

Operation Morningstar

"Children shouldn't be traveling without adults—it's too dangerous these days."

That's what the five Mueller children keep hearing as they make their way across war-torn Germany in search of their father and three younger sisters.

World War Two has just ended, and Katrina, Rudy, Heidi, Helga, and Volfie have just five days to reach their father and sisters before they leave for America. The Muellers have mapped out their journey, and if they stick to their schedule, they should make it. What they haven't planned for are road blocks, unfriendly American soldiers, and spending a night in jail. They have very little food and money, and only their feet to move them. Their hearts are set on finding their father and sisters, but will they reach them in time?

"Please, God!" Katrina prays, "Please help us!"

Based on a true story, *Operation Morningstar* is an exciting adventure you won't want to miss!

Be sure to read all three books in the
Chronicles of Courage series:
A Better Tomorrow?
Operation Morningstar
Gold in the Garden

ChariotVICTOR
PUBLISHING
A DIVISION OF COOK COMMUNICATIONS

Home on Stoney Creek

"Kentucky! Why do we have to move to Kentucky?"

The cry for freedom is spreading throughout the colonies calling many people to war, but not Sarah's family. The cry they hear leads them to a new, untamed wilderness called Kentucky.

Sleeping on pine boughs covered with deerskins, having no one her age to talk to, fighting off pig-eating bears—Kentucky doesn't feel much like freedom to Sarah. She can't understand why God didn't answer her prayers to stay in Virginia, but she vows she'll return some day.

Wanda Luttrell was raised and still lives on the banks of Stoney Creek. Wanda and her husband have shared their home on Stoney Creek with their five children.

Be sure to read all the books in Sarah's Journey:
Home on Stoney Creek
Stranger in Williamsburg
Reunion in Kentucky
Also available as an audio book:
Home on Stoney Creek

Chariot VICTOR
◆ P U B L I S H I N G ◆
A DIVISION OF COOK COMMUNICATIONS

Stranger in Williamsburg

"A spy? Gabrielle Can't be a spy!"

The American Revolution is in full swing, and Sarah Moore is caught right in the middle of it. When she returned to Virginia to live with her aunt's family and learn from their tutor, she certainly had no plans to get involved with a possible spy.

With a war going on, her family back in Kentucky, and people choosing sides all around her, Sarah has begun to wonder if she can trust anyone—even God.

Wanda Luttrell was raised and still lives on the banks of Stoney Creek. Wanda and her husband have shared their home on Stoney Creek with their five children.

Be sure to read all the books in Sarah's Journey:
Home on Stoney Creek
Stranger in Williamsburg
Reunion in Kentucky
Also available as an audio book:
Home on Stoney Creek

ChariotVICTOR
◀ P U B L I S H I N G ▶
A DIVISION OF COOK COMMUNICATIONS

Grandma's Attic Series

Pieces of Magic

Remember when you were a child—when all the world was new, and the smallest object a thing of wonder? Arleta Richardson remembers: the funny wearable wire contraption hidden in the dusty attic, the century-old schoolchild's slate which belonged to Grandma, an ancient trunk filled with quilt pieces—each with its own special story—and the button basket, a miracle of mysteries. And best of all was the remarkable grandmother who made magic of all she touched, bringing the past alive as only a born storyteller could.

Here are those marvelous tales—faithfully recalled for the delight of young and old alike, a touchstone to another day when life was simpler, perhaps richer; when the treasures of family life and love were passed from generation to generation by a child's questions . . . and the legends that followed enlarged our faith.

Arleta Richardson has written the beloved Grandma's Attic series as well as the Orphans' Journey series. She lives in California where she continues writing and public speaking.

Be sure to read all the books from Grandma's Attic:

In Grandma's Attic
More Stories from Grandma's Attic
Still More Stories from Grandma's Attic
Treasure from Grandma

Chariot VICTOR
PUBLISHING
A DIVISION OF COOK COMMUNICATIONS

The Grandma's Attic Novels

At home in North Branch— what could be better?

The Grandma's Attic Novels bring you the story of Mabel O'Dell's young adult years as she becomes a teacher, wife, and mother. Join Mabel and her best friend, Sarah Jane, as they live, laugh, and learn together. They rise to each occasion they meet with their usual measure of hilarity, anguish, and newfound insights, all the while learning more of what it means to live a life of faith.

Arleta Richardson has written the beloved Grandma's Attic series as well as the Orphans' Journey series. She lives in California where she continues writing and public speaking.

Be sure to read all the Grandma's Attic novels:

Away from Home
A School of Her Own
Wedding Bells Ahead
At Home in North Branch
New Faces, New Friends
Stories from the Growing Years

Chariot VICTOR
◀ P U B L I S H I N G ▶
A DIVISION OF COOK COMMUNICATIONS

Parents

Are you looking for fun ways to bring the Bible to life for your children?

ChariotVictor Publishing has hundreds of books, toys, games, and videos that help teach your children the Bible and show them how to apply it to their everyday lives.

Look for these educational, inspirational, and fun products at your local Christian bookstore.